"Bad things hap
You can't save th

"Nobody knows that softly. "But if we found this guy, and if we could find even one person whose life he's ruined, then maybe, just maybe, that would set the past right."

"Nothing—and no one—can set the past right." Dillon shook his head. "Not you, and certainly not me."

"We can," she insisted.

"Don't you get it? There is no 'we.'" He reached for her shoulders, heard her gasp when he pulled her close. "This is as close to *we* as it gets."

He dropped his mouth down on hers, his intention solely to intimidate. Whatever it took to send her packing. She might not realize it, he told himself, but he was doing her a big favor. When she gasped, he parted her lips with his tongue and plundered, waited for her to pull away, waited for her to strike him and call him a bastard.

When she did none of those things, just held very still in his hands, he knew he'd made a serious tactical error.

BARBARA McCAULEY

has written more than thirty novels for Silhouette
Books. She lives in Southern California with her own
handsome hero husband, Frank, who makes it easy
to believe in and write about the magic of romance.
Barbara's stories have won and been nominated for
numerous awards, including the prestigious RITA
Award® from the Romance Writers of America, Best
Desire of the Year from *Romantic Times* and Best Short
Contemporary from the National Reader's Choice
Awards. Her work has also appeared on the *USA TODAY*
bestseller list.

Visit Barbara at her Web site: www.barbaramccauley.com.

BARBARA McCAULEY

BLACKHAWK LEGACY

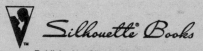

Published by Silhouette Books

America's Publisher of Contemporary Romance

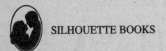 SILHOUETTE BOOKS

BLACKHAWK LEGACY

ISBN 0-373-21849-4

Copyright © 2004 by Barbara Joel

THE BLACKHAWKS

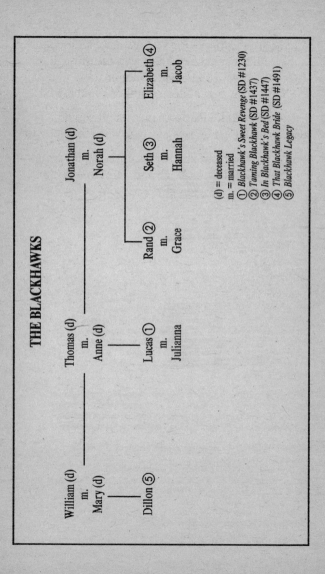

William (d)
m.
Mary (d)

Thomas (d)
m.
Anne (d)

Jonathan (d)
m.
Norah (d)

Dillon ⑤

Lucas ①
m.
Julianna

Rand ②
m.
Grace

Seth ③
m.
Hannah

Elizabeth ④
m.
Jacob

(d) = deceased
m. = married
① *Blackhawk's Sweet Revenge* (SD #1230)
② *Taming Blackhawk* (SD #1437)
③ *In Blackhawk's Bed* (SD #1447)
④ *That Blackhawk Bride* (SD #1491)
⑤ *Blackhawk Legacy*

To Melissa Jeglinski, for your patience and support,
and for sweating bullets with me through
every RITA Award® nomination.
You are the best editor an author could ask for!

To Sandra Paul—thanks for all you do
and for nudging me back on track when I lose my way.

And to my brilliant and beautiful Vegas plot group—
Debbi Rawlins, Jo Leigh and Barbara Ankrum.
You guys rock.

Chapter 1

Midnight jerked him from the dream.

Dillon Blackhawk lay on his back, damp sheets clutched in his fists, sucking air into his lungs. As always, it took him a moment to remember where he was. Which city, which town. Whose bed.

Not that it mattered. They were all the same to him. Different faces, perhaps, different jobs, but still, the same.

Midnight. He closed his eyes again. Always midnight.

Dragging a hand through hair he'd neglected to cut in several months, Dillon sat on the edge of the mattress, waiting for his heart to slow. Like a drum, it pounded heavy in his chest, in his head...*boom...boom...boom...* An ancient, primitive beat. Hollow, deep, foreboding.

There'd be no sleep now. Dillon had learned that much in the past sixteen years. He'd fought it at first. It was in Dillon's blood to fight. Warrior blood, passed proudly down from generation to generation. Pure Cherokee blood.

But the "mind creatures," as his grandfather had called the dream demons, did not fight fair. Cloaked in animal skins, they crept silently in through the darkness. Like shadows, they slipped under and around the strongest defenses, stirring the memories, awakening feelings that Dillon had long ago closed off. He'd managed to hold the creatures at bay, but for the past three weeks, they'd been relentless. Raiding his sleep, invading his dreams. Whispering.

Damn them to hell.

Naked, Dillon rose and stepped over the big dog sleeping at the foot of the bed. Bowie lifted his head briefly, then settled back down again with a sigh. The animal was accustomed to his master's middle of the night risings, and he simply accepted it as part of their routine.

Dillon moved through the darkness into the small bathroom, but didn't bother to turn on the light. The tile was cool under his feet, a relief from the blistering heat of the West Texas summer. Light from a half moon spilled through the open bathroom window and washed the room in shades of gray. He splashed cold water on his face, then gripped the sides of the chipped porcelain sink and rolled his head back. Staring up at the ceiling, he listened to the *drip…drip…drip* of the faucet and breathed in the tangy scent of herbs drifting in from Maria Guadalupe's garden. Cilantro, chili peppers. Rosemary and basil.

For the past six months Dillon had rented a room—a converted garage—behind his landlady's small brick house. Maria, a widow with graying temples, a stout build and a thick waist, loved to cook as much as she loved to eat. Every Sunday she would send her grandson, nine-year-old Juan, with a basket of still warm chili rellenos and homemade tortillas. Juan would insist that his grandmother would beat him if Dillon did not accept the food. Though Dillon knew that Maria raised her voice on occasion, he also knew she would never strike her only grandchild. She'd raised the boy by herself since he was six and little Juan, with his big brown eyes and ready smile, was Maria's greatest joy.

So Dillon silently accepted the lie, just as he accepted the basket, but other than occasional home repairs for his landlady, he offered nothing in return. He had nothing to offer. Not to the Guadalupes, or to anyone else.

He looked in the mirror over the sink, but only a shadowed face without features stared back. Perhaps that was why the dreams had been so frequent lately, he thought. Maybe, without even realizing it, he had been moving too close to the line he never crossed. Wanting things he had no business wanting. Maybe that was why he'd felt an uneasiness these past few days, a persistent prickling on the back of his neck.

A wariness that something, or someone, was coming.

Dillon swiped at the drops of water on his face and chest, then raked both hands through his hair. Tomorrow was Friday. Payday. After he gave Maria this month's rent, he'd blow whatever was left on beer and a few games of pool. A woman would help ease the tension, too, he figured. God knew he'd been without female companionship for way too long.

Cold beer and hot sex. What better solution for a good night's sleep?

Satisfied with that thought, Dillon went back to bed and waited for the morning.

At the edge of the small town, the bar sat alone. Lightbulbs strung from phone poles glowed dimly over the weed-infested dirt-and-gravel parking lot. On top of the flat roof that slanted downward from the front of the wooden building, a yellow neon sign flickered Backwater Saloon.

Hardly an original name, Rebecca Blake thought as she parked her little white sedan between two large, dusty pickup trucks, but it certainly fit the bill.

Resolute, Texas. Population 2,346.

After driving across more than five hundred miles of sparse, flat highways and dusty backroads, this is where she'd finally ended up. Resolute looked like most of the other small towns Rebecca had driven through since she'd flown into the airport in Midland. One long main street, no stop lights, brick buildings circa 1920 and at least one bar, if not two, where locals gathered after work.

According to the travel guide Rebecca had read, Resolute, like so many other Texas towns, had prospered in the height of the oil boom days after a rancher drilling for water hit black gold instead. Though the boom was gone today, enough oil still flowed to sustain a small refinery and provide income to keep the quiet little town on the map.

The Backwater Saloon, however, was anything but quiet. Even with her windows rolled up, Rebecca could hear the pulse of country-western music when the Old West–style saloon doors opened and two men walked out onto the wooden sidewalk. Laughing, they both lit cigarettes and leaned against a rail while they smoked. Their conversation was animated, but appeared friendly, their clothing nearly identical: jeans, boots, striped button-up work shirts with sleeves rolled to the elbows. The only difference between them was that one wore a baseball cap, the other a cowboy hat.

Rebecca had seen more denim, cowboy hats and cowboy boots in the past three days than she had in her entire twenty-eight years. It wasn't that people in Boston didn't wear jeans. Of course they did. She owned several pairs herself. But here in West Texas, it was *how* they wore their denim that was different—as if they owned it. With the same acceptance and confidence that royalty wore their crowns. Here, denim had nothing to do with fashion or fads, and everything to do with practical.

Here—unless you were a cow—a brand meant nothing. A blonde suddenly popped out of the double doors like a stripper out of a cake, her red skirt short enough to get her arrested in most states and her white tank top tight enough to cut off circulation. Her cowboy boots were trimmed with red, white and blue rhinestones. The best word to describe the woman's hair was *big*. She curled up against the taller of the two men, the one wearing a cowboy hat, and then they all three turned and shuffled back into the bar.

Rebecca had never been in a place like the Backwater Saloon, had never even *seen* a place like it before she'd come to Texas. She'd be lying if she didn't admit, at least to herself, that she was afraid. Good God, she was terrified. Walking into a seedy working man's bar by herself, on a crowded Friday night, was hardly the most intelligent thing she'd ever done. If anything, it was just plain stupid. Or crazy.

Both, she decided.

She could only imagine what her sister and brother would say if they knew where she was and what she was doing. Melanie would rant and rave and try to reason with her. Sean, on the other hand, would most likely kill her himself.

But she couldn't let worrying about her family stop her now. She'd come much too far, had waited much too long already. Like it or not—and she didn't—she'd do this tonight.

Dragging a fortifying breath into her lungs, Rebecca opened her car door and stepped out, immediately felt the heavy slap of the evening's heat and humidity. Though she'd confined her shoulder-length hair into a neat ponytail, several loose strands were already curling in protest against the hot, damp air. Out of nerves more than vanity, she straightened the collar of her long-sleeved pink blouse and adjusted the belt on her tailored black slacks.

You can do this, she told herself, then slung the leather strap of her small purse over her shoulder and closed her car door. She'd taken no more than two steps when a huge, snarling mass of sharp teeth and thick fur lunged at her from the bed of the pickup truck she'd parked beside.

Stifling a scream, Rebecca jumped back against the hood of her car, realized with a great deal of relief that the dog was leashed in the bed of the truck. The animal, who looked part grizzly bear, part shepherd, continued to bark.

"Good dog." Gravel crunched under the heels of Rebecca's flats as she slowly backed away. "Nice dog. Stay."

With a low growl, then a soft *woof,* the dog sat, its black eyes wary. Heart hammering, Rebecca turned and picked her way across the dirt parking lot, then stepped onto the wooden sidewalk. A sign over the entrance said No Dogs Or Lizards Allowed.

Since the sign said nothing about third grade teachers from Boston, Rebecca pushed through the double doors.

Inside, a thick cloud of cigarette smoke wrapped itself around her neck like a hand and squeezed while cold air blasted her hot, damp skin. Over the din of conversation and country-western music she recognized as a Willie Nelson song, pool balls clacked from a corner table. Colorful neon beer signs buzzed from every wall, bathing the interior in soft glows of yellow and red and blue.

When she took another step, the room—except for Willie's wailing—went completely still.

It seemed as if every head had swiveled toward her at the same moment. *This is it,* Rebecca thought, and swallowed the thick lump of fear in her throat. *I'm going to die.*

Though it was probably only a few seconds, it felt like a lifetime before the conversations slowly started up again, as did the game of pool. Even though she knew everyone was still watching her, Rebecca released the breath she'd been holding, then made her way to the bar and slid onto the only available stool. To her left, a slender young man with Elvis Presley sideburns and a long, hawkish nose slid her a curious look, while an elderly man to her right touched the brim of his white cowboy hat and smiled wide, giving his face the appearance of cracked leather.

"How do," he said in a voice as dry and gravelly as the parking lot outside. "Elton Potter."

"Mr. Potter." Rebecca managed a weak smile. "Rebecca Blake."

"Folks just call me Elton," the man said. "We ain't fancy around here."

Rebecca glanced around the smoky room, noted the sawdust on the wood-planked floor, a mounted buffalo head over the pool table and a six-foot-long diamond-backed rattlesnake skin stretched out over the sign leading to the restrooms.

No kidding, Elton.

A bartender suddenly appeared, wiping a glass with a towel while he stared at her. He was short, with a flattened nose and arms the size of an oak tree. "What can I get you?"

"Chardonnay, please."

The man to her left snickered, but when the bartender shot him a look, the man cleared his throat and hunched over the beer in his hand.

Rebecca noticed a sign over the back of the bar that said Don't Mess With Texas Or Lester. Apparently, this was Lester.

The bartender pulled out a dusty bottle of white wine from under the bar, wiped it down and opened it, then filled a whiskey glass. He shoved it across the battered, wooden counter and as an afterthought, laid a white cocktail napkin beside the glass. "Twenty dollars."

"For a glass of wine?" Rebecca blurted out, then cursed her own loose tongue.

"For the bottle." Lester folded his beefy arms

across his chest. "And for whatever else it is you're here looking for."

The man certainly didn't mince words, Rebecca thought, then took a sip of the warm chardonnay. And choked. She might as well have bought a bottle of vinegar.

It didn't matter. She hadn't come here for the fine wine and exemplary service.

Pushing the glass away, she reached into her purse, then pulled out two twenties and a pen. She wrote on the napkin and shoved it back across the counter.

Both Elton and Elvis stretched their necks to see what she'd written, but the bartender's meaty hand snatched the napkin away. After he glanced at it, he looked back up at Rebecca.

"Never heard of him." Lester crumpled the napkin and threw it in a trash can.

"Who?" Elton and Elvis both asked eagerly at the same time.

When Lester gave the men a look that could have lasered through steel, Rebecca couldn't help but wonder why. If the bartender truly didn't recognize the name, why would he be making an effort to shut Elton and Elvis up?

Lester glanced back at Rebecca. "So why you looking for this guy?"

"It's a personal matter."

"Yeah?" Lester gave her a hard, bland look, then spread his hands on the bar and leaned in closer. "How personal?"

She didn't like the man's tone or suggestion one little bit, but Rebecca wasn't looking for an invitation to Thanksgiving dinner. Maybe this man knew something and maybe he didn't. She wasn't leaving until she knew for sure.

"I'm a friend of the family." She reached in her purse and pulled out another twenty. "Maybe you could ask around."

Without changing expression, the bartender stared at the money, but said nothing.

"I'll just use the ladies' room while you think about it." Rebecca slid off the bar stool, felt the crunch of sawdust under her shoes. "Watch my wine for me, will you, Elton?"

The old man grinned with pleasure. "Sure thing, miss."

Once again, the beat of the room paused and slowed when she made her way across the room. Still, she kept her head up, her shoulders back and her gaze straight. She didn't hurry, but she didn't stroll, either. She made eye contact with a few of the other patrons, men and women, but didn't hold it. If she'd learned anything from teaching eight-year-olds, it was never, ever, to show fear. The slightest shudder, the tiniest tremble, and any control she might have would be shredded, then tossed about like confetti.

A couple of the men nodded politely at her. Rebecca nodded back, but she didn't smile, knowing that the women in the bar were already wary— staring at her as if she were an alien female come to beam their menfolk up to the mother ship.

But there was only one man she'd come here looking for. Only one man she was remotely interested in. She'd zigzagged across West Texas from one small oil town to another, hoping, praying, that she'd find him. Something in Lester's eyes told her that, finally, she'd hit pay dirt.

In spite of her nerves, excitement fluttered in her stomach.

She cleared the doorway leading to the restrooms. The room on the left had a picture of a cowboy on the door, the room to the right, a cowgirl. Rebecca didn't go inside. Instead, she waited a moment, then peeked back around the corner.

Lester was gone.

She scanned the room, then spotted the bartender standing beside a tall-backed booth on the other side of the bar. She couldn't see who was sitting there, but she watched Lester pull a wad of paper out of his apron pocket and lay it on the table. Unless she missed her guess, it was the napkin Lester had tossed in the trash. The bartender nodded a couple of times, then glanced over his shoulder toward the restrooms. Rebecca's heart slammed against her ribs, and she quickly ducked out of sight.

Was it him? she wondered. Part of her desperately wanted it to be, *needed* it to be. But another part of her was terrified that it was.

She felt like the woman in a horror movie who hears a sound coming from the basement. It was crazy to go down there, who in their right mind *would* go down there? The voice of reason in her head, like an audience in a theater, was screaming at her to run, telling her she was a fool.

Rebecca jumped when the ladies' bathroom door swung open. Laughter and a cloud of heavy cologne preceded the two women who tumbled through the door. Rebecca recognized one of the women as the busty blonde who'd popped through the bar's swinging doors and spoken to the men out front. The brunette beside the blonde wore a red cropped top that showed a lot of bare midriff, a short denim skirt, and red snakeskin cowboy boots. Both women were obviously graduates of the Tammy Faye cosmetology school.

The blonde slid a long, hard look over Rebecca, then raised one interested, but heavily penciled brow. "You lost, honey?"

"Not if this is the ladies' room," Rebecca said, smiling.

The blonde seemed to assess Rebecca's answer and accept it. Her red lips curved into a bright smile. "Not sure about the lady part," she replied, her Texas accent thick, "but if you got to sit down to pee, you're in the right place."

The brunette snorted in laughter. "That's a good one, Dixie. You should do stand-up."

"That's what the guys do," Dixie replied and broke into giggles herself. "Stand up."

The two women laughed so hard, they had to hold on to each other so they wouldn't fall over. Knowing that it never hurt to be friendly to the natives, especially the female ones, Rebecca forced a laugh herself, then watched the women toddle off.

Releasing the breath she'd been holding, Rebecca stepped into the restroom, was thankful it was empty. There were three wooden stalls, though one had an Out Of Order sign on it. The thick scent of sweet cologne and musty tile hung in the air, and the white single-sink countertop was marked with cigarette burns. The walls, desperately in need of paint, vibrated from the blaring jukebox.

Rebecca stared at herself in the mirror over the sink. The past six months had changed her, she thought. Maybe not on the outside. Outside, she supposed no one would notice any difference in her. But inside, where it really mattered, she didn't know who she was anymore.

She'd come a long way to find out. No matter what happened, she wouldn't quit now.

Dillon knew the second the woman had walked into the Backwater Saloon. Not only because beer bottles had frozen in mid-air and the pool game had stopped, not only because every head had swiveled and stared.

But because he'd *felt* her.

He'd felt her presence, knew before he'd even turned to look that she'd come here for him. All day, he'd felt her shadow beside him, had tried to shrug it off as lack of sleep the night before. But in his gut, he'd known. The dreams had warned him, but he hadn't listened closely enough this time. If he had, he would have packed up and left this morning.

I must be getting old.

It didn't matter, Dillon told himself and tossed back a swig from the bottle of beer in his hand. It wasn't the first time his past had risen out of the ashes. It probably wouldn't be the last, either. It did surprise him that they'd sent a woman to come find him this time, though, especially one who looked like she'd just stepped out of Miss Prim's Prep

School. He could picture her gliding stiffly across a room with a book balanced on her head—probably Dickinson or Brontë, Dillon decided. She had a face that would match one of those Victorian writers' heroines: high cheekbones, skin milkmaid white, thick, dark brown strands of curls framing her heart-shaped face and wide eyes.

She was tall—at least five foot eight—and slender, too. Dillon had the feeling there were some serious curves going on under her black tailored slacks and long-sleeved blouse. He'd spotted the fear in her gaze when she'd walked into the bar, but she'd managed to hold her own, simply glanced across the room as if she owned it, then walked with purpose to the counter and slid onto a stool. He'd actually even felt a flicker of admiration she hadn't shriveled under the intense scrutiny of the crowd.

She fit in like a cactus in a Jacuzzi, but whoever she was, and whatever she wanted, he'd send her pretty little ass on her pretty little way.

Dillon stared at the wrinkled napkin Lester had given him. He was absolutely certain he'd never met this woman before, unless maybe he'd been blind drunk at the time. A possibility, he supposed, but highly unlikely. Even blind drunk, he'd have remembered this one.

Which meant Peter had sent her, Dillon thought,

though the man had never sent a woman before. Dammit. He should have left while she was in the restroom.

But he was comfortable sitting right where he was and besides, he still had half a beer. He'd be damned if he'd leave before he finished it.

And if he were really being honest, he was more than a little curious. He stared at the crumpled napkin she'd written his name on, then turned it over and set his damp beer bottle on top. Either she wasn't very bright, or she had *cojones*. More than the men who had preceded her. They would have found him at work, or waited outside his house rather than set foot in a place like this.

Whatever, he thought, since she'd apparently gone to such lengths to find him, he decided he'd at least hear her out.

He knew she was standing next to him now. Even before she spoke, he caught her scent. Light and floral, slightly sweet. The kind of scent a man wanted not only to smell, but to taste.

"Dillon Blackhawk?"

He ignored her question and the velvet-smooth sound of her voice and took another slow pull on his beer. Dillon knew that everyone in the bar was watching him, dammit. Waiting. He lowered the bottle in his hand, then rudely slid his gaze up her body, pausing to stare at her breasts. Full, round, just the right size for a man's hand, he thought.

He watched her stiffen at his lecherous inspection, then she tilted her chin up and repeated, "Are you Dillon Blackhawk?"

There was an icy chill in her voice now. With reluctance, he glanced up and met her gaze. Her eyes, a deep, startling green, caught him slightly off guard. "Who wants to know?"

She slid into the booth across from him. "My name is Rebecca Blake."

The name meant nothing, but she had a hell of a mouth, Dillon noted. Lush and full, tipped up slightly at the corners. When he didn't respond, she reached into the black purse slung over her shoulder and pulled out a photograph, then slid it across the table, facing him. It took him a moment to realize that it was his own high school graduation picture. God, had he really ever been that young? Other than his driver's license and the army, it was the last time he could even remember having his picture taken. What the hell was this woman doing with it?

Still, he showed no reaction.

"I need to know I have the right man," she said evenly.

"Depends on what you're looking for, darlin'," Dillon said with a lift of one brow.

Those incredible lips of hers pressed into a thin line, and her already stiff back straightened even more. "Are you Dillon Takota Blackhawk?"

Her question was a verbal blow that caught him straight in the gut. *Takota.* His middle name wasn't even on his birth certificate. He'd been given the name later by his grandfather. No one knew it— no one living, anyway.

"Lady—" Dillon narrowed his gaze "—you've got exactly five seconds to tell me who you are and what you want."

Chapter 2

It was one thing to look for the man, Rebecca thought, keeping her hands under the table so he couldn't see that they were shaking. It was quite another to find him.

Rebecca stared at Dillon Blackhawk, tried to find some resemblance to the seventeen-year-old in the photo who'd been offered scholarships at nearly every college he'd applied to, and a half dozen where he hadn't, then seemed to drop off the face of the earth after his high school graduation. She tried to find even a remote likeness to the teenager who'd been the captain of the football team and valedictorian of his class.

But there were no traces of that boy in the man sitting across from her, Rebecca thought. No devil-may-care tilt of his head, no charming smile, no glint of mischief in the eyes.

This Dillon Blackhawk could have been carved from granite. Not just the broad stretch of solid muscle under the navy blue T-shirt he wore, but his features were blunt and angular, too, his mouth hard and firm, his intense eyes nearly as black as his long, thick hair. Rebecca might have thought she had the wrong man except for the structure of his face. The strong cheekbones, the square jaw, the bold slash of dark brow. Bronze skin. All gave testament not only to his Native American heritage, but to the Blackhawk family itself.

"I already told you who I am." She knew her name would mean nothing to him. "Why I'm here is a little more complicated."

"Tell you what," Dillon said, his tone sounding as bored as it was annoyed, "you keep the words under three syllables and talk real slow. Maybe I'll be able to follow along."

Somehow, Rebecca had never visualized her meeting with Dillon to be quite so difficult. Had never visualized *him* to be so difficult. Though she hadn't exactly expected him to throw out the welcome mat for her, she certainly hadn't expected him to be so brusque, either.

The sound of glass breaking, then a string of ear-burning curse words made Rebecca flinch. She glanced over her shoulder at the commotion by the pool table in the opposite corner, noticed two men arguing, then a third man stepped between them and pushed them apart. She looked back at Dillon, who seemed completely oblivious to the altercation. "Is there someplace quiet we can go to talk?"

"Darlin', if we go somewhere quiet, we won't be talking." His black eyes glittered. "We'll just skip straight to the good stuff."

If he was trying to provoke her, Rebecca thought, he was doing one hell of a job. Six months ago, she probably would have run away—no, she corrected herself, not *probably*. Six months ago, she would have been home grading papers, listening to Mozart instead of some twangy female singing about her cheating man.

Rebecca met Dillon's dark gaze and held it. "There's no reason to be rude."

"I'm being rude?" He raised a brow and snorted. "Bribery and lies are what I consider rude, Miss Blake. Go back to Peter and tell him the next time he sends a woman to bother me while I'm drinking, she better be a hooker."

It was one thing to be rude, Rebecca thought, and quite another to be vulgar. She lifted her chin and frowned at Dillon. "If the bribery refers to the money I gave the bartender, I was merely buying information. I haven't lied about anything, and I have no idea who Peter is."

"Now you're lying about lying," Dillon said tightly, then stood. "This conversation is over."

"Wait."

Without thinking, she reached out and took hold of his forearm. His skin was hot under her hand, his muscles like forged steel. He towered over her, and she knew with an easy cuff of his large hand he could smack her away like a pesty gnat. When he glared down at her, she also knew she should let go—a wiser person certainly would have. But no matter what the consequences, she couldn't. She felt him tense under her touch, watched his eyes narrow darkly.

She didn't know what else to do, so she just started rambling in a whisper, "You were born in Wolf River County, Texas, thirty-three years ago, an only child. Your father was William Blackhawk, your mother Mary. When you were eight, you had a border collie named Arrow who slept in your room at night. When you were nine you broke your right foot on a wild horse roundup. You left Wolf River the day after you graduated high school. Your mother died two months later, your father died two years ago in a small plane accident. You have forty million dollars in trust, but you live like a pauper, jumping from small town to small town, oil field to oil field, leaving no forwarding address."

In a millisecond, Dillon's eyes went from burning cold to piercing hot. A thunderbolt of barely controlled fury shot through his body up Rebecca's arm. The intensity of the emotion was like a strong electrical current, locking her hand to his arm. If she'd wanted to, she couldn't have let go.

Dillon stared at her for a long, heart-stopping moment. It shocked Rebecca that she didn't melt under the heat of his gaze. She hadn't meant to blurt out so much, but between her exasperation and desperation, she'd simply lost it.

"Wish I could say it's been a pleasure, Miss Blake." Dillon yanked his arm away. "But it hasn't. And you just wasted sixty bucks."

He turned and walked away without so much as a backward glance. The sea of people seemed to part as Dillon made his way through the bar, a couple of the men said something to Dillon about beer and a game of pool, but he didn't respond, just kept moving toward the entrance.

Clearly, she'd been dismissed.

Rebecca watched Dillon disappear out the front door, then she set her teeth and narrowed her eyes. She *couldn't* let him just walk away. At least not until he'd completely heard her out. If he didn't like it, that was just too damn bad. Tugging the strap of her purse over her shoulder, she made her way through the people and hurried after him.

Outside, she quickly scanned the dark parking lot, then spotted him opening the door of a black truck. The one with the snarling dog. *Terrific.* That's all she needed to end her perfect evening. Another encounter with Cujo.

Not that Dillon was any easier.

"Dillon!" She hurried across the parking lot, but he didn't respond or even slow down, just climbed into the cab of his pickup and closed the door. She broke into a run, managed to reach his passenger door and open it as he started his engine. The animal leashed in the truck bed leaped out at her and caught the sleeve of her blouse between his fangs. Rebecca heard the sound of cloth ripping as she dove into the cab.

Dillon stared at her, his dark eyes disbelieving, then glanced down at her torn shirt. "What the *hell* do you think you're doing?"

"I need to talk to you," she said between gulps of air and fear that the still barking dog would lunge straight through the cab's back window. "About your family."

"I don't have any family. Bowie, off! Sit!" Dillon shifted in the front seat and looked at the dog. Still growling, the animal sat, but kept its eyes locked on the intruder. "You said it yourself. My mother and father are both dead, and I have no sisters or brothers. Now either tell me what the hell you want, or get the hell out of my truck."

"You do have family," Rebecca insisted. She had to start somewhere, and for the moment, Lucas was the best place. "A cousin, Lucas. He's three years older than you."

"Oh, right. Lucas. So that's the scam, is it?" Dillon shut off his engine. "My long lost cousin wants to borrow a few bucks, just until he gets back on his feet. Right?"

"No." Confused, she shook her head. "This isn't a scam. I can—"

"Why didn't you say it was money you wanted, Miss Blake?" Dillon reached across the cab and took hold of Rebecca's chin. Stroking her jawline, he lowered his voice. "Since you're apparently the broker here, I'm sure we can negotiate some kind of a deal."

She slapped his hand away, which set off the dog again. "You are the crudest man I've ever met," she said through clenched teeth. "Dammit, will you get it through your thick head this *isn't* about money. Lucas doesn't need, or want your money. And neither do Rand, Seth or Elizabeth."

He went very still, then his eyes narrowed to thin slits. "Is this some kind of sick joke?"

She certainly hadn't intended to tell him this way. But why should she be surprised? Nothing at all had happened the way she'd intended.

"They're alive, Dillon," she said quietly, rubbing her chin. "Rand. Seth. Elizabeth. I know you think your cousins died in a car accident twenty-four years ago. But they're alive."

"The hell they are," Dillon snapped. "I went to their funerals. I stood next to their open graves and watched their caskets lower into the ground. Don't tell me they didn't die, lady. I was *there.*"

"This is complicated," she said, knowing herself what an understatement that was. "But if you give me a chance, I can—"

"You're out of chances, sweetheart." He reached across her and opened the door. "I don't know what it is you want, and frankly I don't give a damn. Now get the hell out of my truck!"

Between Dillon and the dog both snarling at her, Rebecca had no choice but to jump out of the truck. She stumbled backward into her own car, managed to steady herself on the hood.

Dillon's truck roared to life, and he shot forward. The back wheels spun, spewing dirt and gravel.

Tears burned Rebecca's eyes as he drove off.

Damn you, Dillon Blackhawk. Damn you, damn you, damn you!

She watched the red glow of his taillights as he drove down main street. When he turned left at the end of town and disappeared, she sank back against her car and dropped her head in her hands.

She considered walking away. It would be so easy to just get in her car and drive back to her motel room, then in the morning go to the airport and take the first flight out. Let the miserable man rot away in his miserable life.

But whether he liked it or not—and he obviously didn't—he was part of this. She wouldn't go back to her motel tonight, and she wouldn't go home tomorrow.

She rolled up the sleeves of her blouse to hide the torn fabric, dragged a hand through her hair, then turned and headed back into the bar.

The lights were still on in the Guadalupe living room when Dillon parked in the driveway. It was only nine o'clock and he knew his landlady would still be watching television. The woman was a reality show fanatic, and recorded her favorites during the week, then watched them a second time on Friday night. Maria's all-time favorite was the one with the bachelor who starts out dating sixteen women, then keeps weeding them out until he's left with one.

Maria had told him once she was going to send

his picture to the popular show, that she thought he was sexier and better looking than any man they'd had on the series before. He'd frowned at her, but she'd frowned right back and folded her beefy arms. "It is against the laws of nature for a man who looks like you to be alone," Maria had said with the utmost authority. "You need a woman. Someone to take care of you. *Uno esposa.* Wait here and I will get my camera. You will be America's next celebrity *soltero.*"

It must have been the expression of sheer terror on his face that had made Maria laugh a moment later. *"Algun dia, mijo,"* she'd said with a sigh. "One day." Not a snowball's chance in hell, he'd thought. He didn't need anyone to take care of him, and he sure as hell didn't need, or want, a wife.

From the back of the truck, Bowie's shrill bark dragged Dillon from his thoughts. He cut the engine, then stepped out of the cab and unleashed the anxious dog. The animal didn't even wait for Dillon to lower the tailgate, but bounded over the side of the truck and raced across the street to the neighbors who owned a pretty little golden retriever named Maggie.

While he waited for Bowie to come back from his rendezvous, Dillon crossed his arms and leaned against his truck, breathed in the scent of climbing jasmine from the house next door, listened to the sound of busy crickets and the whir of Maria's front room window fan. He was too wound up to go inside just yet, anyway, knew that the walls would only press in on him if he did.

It infuriated, and admittedly, confounded him that this woman, Rebecca Blake, had somehow managed to track him down. No one in Resolute, or any of the other numerous places Dillon had lived in the past sixteen years, knew anything about his background. That was exactly the way he wanted it, and exactly the way he intended to keep it.

Dillon's first guess—that Peter had sent Rebecca—had obviously been wrong. As executor of William Blackhawk's estate, Peter Hansen was the only person who knew how to directly contact Dillon. On several occasions—usually when Dillon neglected to return Peter's calls—one of Peter's assistants would eventually show up, needing signatures and approval for various investments and transactions.

But Peter had never sent a woman before. And he'd certainly never send anyone who would dare confront Dillon about his mother and father.

Even the news of William Blackhawk's death had been sent to Dillon by registered mail after a private detective had located him. Peter, in his pragmatic, matter-of-fact manner had simply stated,

Dillon, I regret to inform you that your father was killed in a plane crash over New Mexico two days ago. Services will be held one o'clock Thursday, at Wolf River Community Church. My condolences,

    Peter Hansen, Executor for W.B. Enterprises

Dillon had not attended the funeral, but Peter had sent detailed instructions set forth in William Blackhawk's will and a listing of the assets: fifty thousand acres that comprised the Circle B in Wolf River County, plus other real estate in Texas, California and New Mexico. Stocks and bonds. Mutual funds. Savings accounts. All totaling in excess of forty million dollars, and all Dillon's.

He hadn't taken one red cent.

The Circle B had been closed up since his father's death, and Peter oversaw the vast holdings that now belonged to Dillon. None of it—the money, the land, the corporation—meant a damn thing to him.

But no doubt, Dillon thought, pressing his lips together, it meant something to Miss Rebecca Blake.

The woman's visit had to be some kind of a con—a bad one, to be sure, but a con, nonetheless. Three dead cousins resurrected, miraculously plucked from their graves. All alive and anxious to meet the long-lost cousin they'd barely known. All gathered together for a tearful reunion while bluebirds sang and flowers bloomed.

What a crock.

He had to give points to Miss Blake, though. She'd certainly done her homework. His dog and the broken foot were nice touches, but if she'd dug hard enough—and she obviously had—there had to be a few Circle B ranch hands still around who'd worked for his father when Dillon was a kid. It was easy enough to buy information.

They're alive, Dillon. Rand, Seth and Elizabeth. They didn't die in the accident.

How in the world could she—could *anyone*— in their right mind expect him to believe such a lie? He'd *been* there. He'd only been a kid, but with his own eyes, he'd seen the five open graves, watched the ground slowly swallow each casket as it was lowered into the freshly dug earth. Earth still damp from the storm that had taken Jonathan and Norah Blackhawk and their three children.

Elizabeth, barely three, had been the smallest casket of all. Dillon could still feel his mother tightly squeeze his hand, could hear her quiet sob as that tiny white casket had been lowered into the ground last.

Several feet away, William Blackhawk had stood like a statue dressed in black. Arms folded, back stiff, eyes shadowed behind sunglasses. Crying, Dillon had broken away from his mother, then ran to his father and thrown his arms around his waist. But his father did not move, did not even look down, and a moment later, his mother had pulled her son away and taken him back to the car.

"We must let your father grieve alone, Dillon," his mother had said.

Dillon did not understand what that word meant. He did not understand death. He looked at his father through the car window.

"Why does he stand there like that?" Dillon asked quietly.

His mother stared out at her husband. *"Because he is so very sad."*

Dillon didn't think his father looked sad. He thought he looked angry.

"You must be strong for him right now," Mary Blackhawk said. *"You must be strong for me."*

"I am strong." Dillon sat straighter and lifted his chin high. *"Yesterday I saddled Attilla all by myself."*

But when Dillon looked at the graves again, he didn't feel strong. He was frightened. Only a year ago, his grandfather had died. Now his aunt and uncle and cousins. What if his own mother and father died? Who would take care of him? Where would he live?

"I am so proud of you." Mary hugged him close. *"Promise me you will never leave me."*

"Never."

In the warm comfort of his mother's arms, Dillon forgot his fear. Even dressed in black and with her hair pulled tightly back, he thought his mother was the most beautiful woman in the world. Her eyes were lighter than his own, like the color of mink. The blunt ends of her coal-black hair skimmed the middle of her back. She had the same high cheekbones as he did, but her features were delicate and soft. When she tucked him in at night, she always smoothed the sheets and kissed his cheek.

Tonight he would tell her he was too big to be tucked in. Tonight, and from now on, he would be strong and brave….

The sound of a dog barking snapped Dillon back to the present. He whistled for Bowie, and for a split second, as the animal bounded out of the darkness, it wasn't Bowie Dillon saw. It was another dog—a black and white border collie that had slept at the foot of his bed for twelve years.

Just as quickly, that image was gone and it was Bowie racing across the street, Bowie sitting at his feet, Bowie with his tongue hanging happily out of the side of his big jaws.

Dillon frowned. Rebecca Blake had not only

lied, she'd stirred up memories he'd thought long dead. Memories better left alone.

And that, he thought, pushing away from his truck and heading inside, was unforgivable.

On the penthouse floor of the thirty-two-story luxury apartment building, the man stood at the window and stared out into the night. Behind him, strains of Vivaldi's *Four Seasons* played softly from the high tech sound system. Below him, moonlight danced on the ocean, illuminating the harbor. His baby was moored down there. *The Island Dream.* One hundred seventy-four feet, every square inch was custom made. Six cabins, formal dining and living area, satellite screening room, Jacuzzi. It had taken him three years to have it built exactly the way he wanted, and in two weeks, he would retire there. At fifty-six, he didn't really consider it retirement. Just a change in address.

A permanent change.

He could go anywhere he liked, whenever he liked. Would answer to no one. It had taken him nearly thirty years to achieve his dream, but in exactly one week he would set sail.

Smiling at the thought, he sipped at the snifter in his hand, enjoyed the spicy, smooth slide of twelve-year-old scotch down his throat. One week, and he'd never have to look over his shoulder again. Never have to wonder if he'd covered his tracks well enough. Never have to change his name, his residence or his office. Or his appearance.

Not that he didn't like his new nose and jawline. He thought the sculpting of his face made him look debonair. Even a bit noble. The ladies never complained, he thought, sipping from his glass again. But then, why would they? He enjoyed spending money as much as he enjoyed making it, and a diamond bracelet or new car kept even the most difficult female silent and on her back.

Exactly the way he liked them.

When the phone rang, he ignored it. When it rang again, he frowned. What the hell was he paying his servant for, dammit, if not to handle the mundane, boring tasks in life?

The butler appeared in the doorway a moment later and cleared his throat. "Mr. Edmunds is on the phone, sir. Shall I tell him you're in?"

'Bout damn time. "I'll take it in my office."

He moved into the next room and closed the door, then picked up the phone sitting on top of his glass desk. "Well?"

"I've had a temporary setback."

His hand tightened on the phone. "What the hell do you mean, a temporary setback?"

The man's voice on the other end of the line was

flat, unconcerned. "I was with her until this morning, then I blew out a tire and lost her."

"You work for me because you're supposed to be the best." He could feel the blood pounding in his temple, then took in a slow breath to calm himself. "I'm paying you a lot of fucking money, Edmunds."

"I told you, it's temporary. I know what she's doing and where she's going, and I'm right on her pretty little ass."

"I don't want you on her ass, dammit," he hissed into the phone. "I want you on top of her. I want you in front of her. I want you breathing the same air as her, at the same time. Don't call me again until you've got her."

Slamming the phone down, he tossed back the rest of his scotch, then dragged a hand over his head.

"Goddamn idiot."

He might be annoyed, but he really wasn't worried. Even if the woman found William's kid—and he doubted she would—the chances of him helping her were between slim and none. Other than a stint in the army, Dillon Blackhawk had been slumming around West Texas for the past sixteen years. Even inheriting forty fucking million dollars hadn't enticed him out of his cave. What were the chances he'd come out now?

Zilch, he thought. But still, he knew he could never be too careful. He hadn't worked his ass off for the past twenty-four years to have some witless female suddenly rip his life into shreds. He'd do whatever he had to do to ensure no one interfered.

In one more week, he'd be free of everything. He had plenty of time to do what he needed to do before he set sail. Once he did, there wasn't a soul on earth who could find him.

Chapter 3

Teresa Angelina Bellochio felt the first contraction when she stepped off the bus. No more than a sharp pinch, really, but enough to make her draw in a breath. She wasn't worried. It was too soon to actually be in labor. She was only eight months pregnant and just yesterday, the doctor at the clinic in San Antonio had reassured her that everything was fine and it would be safe to travel short distances.

She'd had no choice but to make the two-hundred-dred-mile bus ride. There'd been nothing for her in San Antonio but heartbreak. Her boyfriend had denied the baby was his and her parents had turned their back on her when she'd refused to have an abortion or give her baby up for adoption. Her father had cursed her, told her that she'd shamed the Bellochio name.

Teresa laid a protective hand on her belly. How could there be shame in such a precious gift? she wondered. It didn't matter to her that she was barely eighteen, or that she would have to work to support herself and her child. She knew it would be hard, but she would die before she gave up her baby. She had made mistakes, yes, but deciding to keep her baby was not one of them.

She glanced around the bus terminal, at the people hurrying by her with their suitcases and backpacks. Strange faces, strange place. She was nervous, but at least she had a job here. It didn't pay much, but it was a chance for a new life. She would never look back on what she'd left behind her. She didn't know what sex her baby was, the one ultrasound she'd had early in her pregnancy had been unclear. But boy or girl, it didn't matter to her. A healthy baby was all she prayed for. She already had her names picked out—Carissa if she had a girl, Cade if she had a boy. They would be happy here, Teresa thought, just the two of them. Even if she couldn't give her child more than love, for now, it would be enough.

Another twinge low in her stomach made Teresa hesitate, but it quickly passed. The doctor had told her it was perfectly normal to experience mild contractions the last few weeks of her pregnancy, and she shouldn't be concerned unless they were strong or consistent or if her water broke. He had also said that most first-time mothers went past their due date. But she was already so big, Teresa hoped her child would be born on the day she'd been told, July twenty-ninth—exactly four weeks from now.

She couldn't wait to hold her baby in her arms. Couldn't wait to kiss his soft cheek. *Soon, my little one,* she thought, picking up her suitcase, then headed for the pay phone outside the terminal. She pulled a slip of paper out of her wallet, then dropped some change into the phone. At the sound of a dial tone, she punched in the number her new employer had given her.

Tenderly, she touched her belly again. *Today is the first day of the rest of our lives,* she thought, smiling.

Scarlet red bougainvillea covered the trellised porch of the small brick house on 324 Via Verde Lane. The front lawn, still damp with early morning dew, was neat and freshly edged, and a stone flower bed of tall, black-eyed Susans and white daisies shared space with colorful stakes of dancing garden angels. In the thick branches of thorned bougainvillea, sparrows fluttered and chirped while a bully scrub jay squawked and greedily picked through seeds in a wooden bird feeder hanging from an eave under the porch.

Parked across the street, her windows rolled down, Rebecca sat in her car and waited.

Except for the repetitive *ch-ch-ch* of a distant oscillating sprinkler, there'd been little activity on Via Verde since she'd arrived at 6:30 a.m. At the far end of the block, a woman wearing a white robe and pink slippers had strolled out and picked up her newspaper. Ten minutes later, on the opposite side of the street, a man wearing gray overalls got into a white plumbing van and drove off.

It was an older neighborhood, most of the houses brick or clapboard. The sidewalks were clean, but cracked from trees planted in the parkway probably forty years earlier. The mailboxes, all traditional metal boxes on four by four wood posts, lined the street like sleepy sentinels.

Rebecca couldn't quite picture Dillon Blackhawk living here. An apartment maybe—or even a mountain cave—but not a quiet family neighborhood. If his truck hadn't been parked in the driveway, she might have thought she'd been given the wrong address.

She looked at the street and number she'd written down on a napkin from the Backwater Saloon.

She'd paid dearly for the information last night—Jose Cuervo shooters with Dixie and her friend, Jennie. Rebecca had followed Dixie's lead with the lime and salt, then tossed back the first shot of tequila. It went down like a fireball. When she'd choked, the women had laughed, then poured her another shot. That one went down much smoother.

The third one she'd barely felt.

Until she'd woken up this morning to the construction crew working inside her head. Two cups of coffee and aspirin had quieted the noise inside her skull, but her eyeballs still felt like they might fall out at any moment. Just in case they did, Rebecca slipped on a pair of sunglasses.

If she never saw another bottle of Jose Cuervo in her life, it would be too soon. Thank goodness Jennie had been designated driver or Rebecca would have had to crawl back to the motel last night. The image of that alone made her head hurt.

She winced at the sound of a dog's shrill bark, then glanced up as Dillon came out of a wooden gate that joined the house to the garage. He wore deep blue sport shorts, a white T-shirt with the sleeves cut off and running shoes. He had an early morning rough-and-tumble look about him. His long black hair was pulled hastily back into a ponytail with a thin, brown leather strap and his dark eyes appeared heavy-lidded. Even in the light of early morning, he looked formidable and completely unapproachable.

He also looked handsome as the devil.

It was easy to picture this man in a loin cloth, she thought. He had the body of a warrior. Solid muscle, long limbs. A body built for speed and power—or the front cover of a men's fitness magazine. Even from across the street, she could see a long, jagged scar on his right thigh.

She tamped down the jolt of lust, reminded herself he was surly and rude and he'd practically shoved her out of his truck last night. No amount of good-looking overcame such appalling behavior, Rebecca thought. She'd take polite and kind and a good sense of humor in a man over handsome any day.

Well, most days, anyway, she amended, watching Dillon press his palms against the fence and stretch his back.

It was obvious he was getting ready for a run and she knew if she didn't move now, she'd miss her opportunity. Opening her car door, she grabbed her purse and the manila folder she'd brought with her, then stepped out. He turned in her direction and frowned. She expected him to turn and go back through the gate, but he surprised her when he simply folded his arms and leaned against the fence, keeping his gaze on her as she approached.

Rebecca swallowed the lump in her throat. Even though she wore long khaki slacks and a white V-neck cotton top, the way he was looking at her made her feel naked.

Back straight, she stood at the edge of the driveway. "I swear to you, I'm not here for money."

When his dog started to bark on the other side of the fence, Rebecca shifted nervously.

"Bowie, quiet," Dillon said without raising his voice. The dog immediately stopped barking. "How did you find me?"

She doubted that Dillon wanted to hear she'd swapped gossip with Dixie and Jennie at the Backwater Saloon. Rebecca had not been specific, but she'd strongly implied that she and Dillon had a history and it hadn't ended well.

Between drinks and sympathetic pats on the hand from Dixie and Jennie, Rebecca had learned that Dillon had lived in Resolute for the past six months, he worked at the refinery and mostly kept to himself, but had dated Ilene Baker, a nurse at a local hospital. Lucky Ilene, Dixie and Jennie had called the woman. There'd been several rumors about the man, none of them proven fact or fiction. One story was that he'd been married, but caught his wife cheating and spent time in prison after he beat the hell out of the guy. Another story was that he had a family, but they all died in a car crash and since he was driving, he blamed himself.

Rebecca's favorite story was that he'd been engaged to a wealthy oil heiress in Dallas, but she'd left him at the altar and he'd never gotten over her.

Rebecca doubted that any of those rumors were true, but she supposed anything was possible. There were several blank years after Dillon had left Wolf River. For all she knew, he could have been married ten times, he could have been in prison, and he certainly could have been ditched at the altar. *That* rumor was easy to believe.

The fact was, she really didn't care.

"There are just over two thousand people in this town, Dillon," Rebecca said with a shrug. "I could have found you just by driving around."

"That's not what I mean." He frowned. "I want to know how you found me at all."

She didn't think this was a good time to tell him a private investigator had been partially involved. "Let's just say it wasn't easy. You move around a lot."

"That's so people like you won't bother me."

"People like me?" she repeated. "You don't know anything about me."

A blue Taurus drove by and the man inside waved at Dillon, who nodded back. "I'm sure it's all very fascinating, sweetheart, but you're interrupting my morning run."

"If you won't listen to me, then talk to Henry Barnes. He's the lawyer in Wolf River who's handled all this. Let him tell you what happened to Rand and Seth and Elizabeth."

"I know what happened," he said through clenched teeth. "I told you, I was at the funeral. I don't know what you or Lucas could possibly hope to gain by fabricating such an elaborate story, and frankly, I don't give a damn."

When he started to move past her, she quickly blocked his way. "Lucas doesn't know I'm here. No one knows."

"You're starting to make me mad, Miss Blake." Dillon's eyes narrowed to slits. "Trust me, you don't want to make me mad."

"I don't give a damn if I make you mad." She didn't care what he did to her anymore. She was just too tired, her head hurt and she was so frustrated she wanted to scream. She leaned back against the fence and closed her eyes. "You can sic your dog on me and bully me some more if it makes you feel like a man, but I'm not going away until you talk to me."

Rebecca's eyes popped open when Dillon placed an arm on either side of her and leaned in. She couldn't breathe, couldn't think, but still she refused to back down. She sucked in a breath and met his gaze.

"I can prove Rand and Seth and Elizabeth are alive," she said quietly. "I have hospital records, DNA tests and an eyewitness account. They all confirm, without a doubt, that your cousins didn't die that night."

"I told you," he said evenly. "I was at the funeral. I saw with my own eyes."

"What did you see?" Rebecca asked. "What *exactly* did you see?"

Reluctantly, he took himself back to that day again, at the mortuary, before the caskets had been closed and brought to the ranch. It was the first time he'd ever seen a dead person. Uncle John, dressed in a gray suit and black tie, laying so still against the white satin lining of his casket. Aunt Norah, her hair dark and shiny against her pale skin. He thought if he touched her, her eyes would open and she'd turn to him with her pretty blue eyes and brilliant smile. Dillon barely knew them, yet at that moment, standing over their coffins, he missed them terribly. He didn't want them to be dead. He didn't want them to go away.

"I *saw* my aunt and uncle," he said tightly. "Before my father closed their caskets, I saw them both."

"But not your cousins," Rebecca said. "You didn't see them, did you?"

His mother had told him he was too young to see his cousins like that, that their souls had gone to heaven and he should pray for them. Every Sunday after that, until the day he left Wolf River, Dillon's mother drove to the private cemetery on the ranch and laid flowers on all five graves.

Dillon brought his gaze level with Rebecca's. She didn't flinch, she didn't even blink. If she was lying, he thought, she was damn good. In the morning light, her eyes were a softer green than last night, with striations of gray that looked like smoke. And suddenly there was something—nothing he could explain or give substance to—something familiar about those eyes.

"Who the hell are you?" he asked.

"I was born Rebecca Alexis Owens," she said. "My mother's name, before she remarried my stepfather, was Rosemary Owens."

"Means nothing to me."

"You called my mother Rosie. You used to love the macaroni and cheese she made for you on Fridays."

Rosie. Something inside Dillon went very still.

Dark red hair. Freckles. A quick smile. When she sang, which was often, she had an Irish lilt to her voice. He remembered she had always smelled like lemon wax.

Dillon had never known the housekeeper's last

name. To him, she was simply Rosie. The woman couldn't have been more than twenty-five when she'd worked at the Circle B. She'd lived in the guest house with her young daughter, and occasionally the little brown-haired girl would wander into the barn, wanting to feed the horses apples or play with the resident cats.

"Becky," Dillon muttered.

"That's what you used to call me, along with Nudnik, Beanpole, and Brat. You put me on your horse one time and walked me around the corral," she said quietly. "You told me to hold tight to the saddle horn so I wouldn't fall."

Dillon didn't remember what he'd said, but he did remember the little girl's giggles when he'd swung her up on his horse. She'd been a scrawny kid, with wild, curly hair and holes in her tennis shoes.

And big, green eyes. The same green eyes he was looking into now. "How can you possibly remember that? You couldn't have been more than four."

"I had just turned five," she said. "And I remember because your father came out of the barn a few minutes later. He was so angry I thought he was going to hit you. I thought I'd done something wrong, and knew that I'd gotten you into trouble. When he pulled me off the horse, I was terrified and ran away."

"If you're bored or have so much extra time on

*your hands to give pony rides to servants' chil-
dren,"* Dillon remembered his father had said after
Becky had run off, *"then I obviously haven't given
you enough chores around here."*

Dillon had spent the last two weeks of his summer vacation mucking stalls, painting the fence
around his mother's garden and cleaning the tack
room, but he knew the extra chores weren't because his father thought his son had too much time
on his hands. It was because Dillon had crossed the
line his father had distinctly drawn between white
and Indian, between rich and poor. William Blackhawk had made it clear that anyone who wasn't
pure blood Native American was inferior. That included little green-eyed girls who liked to play
with kittens and ride ponies.

At the sound of a car starting in the garage next
door, Dillon straightened. The last thing he needed
were the neighbors yammering on about Maria's
tenant standing in the driveway with a pretty brunette at six-thirty in the morning. As it was, Dillon had no doubt that Maria herself, at this very
moment, was watching this little drama unfold
from her kitchen window.

"Please," Rebecca said, her voice strained. "Just
hear me out."

She'd probably chain herself to the fence until
he did, he thought with a sigh. If the only way to

get rid of her was to listen to whatever she was so insistent on telling him, then so be it. But he'd listen without an audience.

Turning, he opened the gate, then looked over his shoulder at her. She still leaned against the fence, watching him, her eyes wide with uncertainty.

It took Rebecca a moment to realize that Dillon was waiting for her to follow him inside. It was one thing to walk into a crowded, public bar, or stand out here in his driveway, and quite another to be alone with the man. Completely alone.

When she hesitated, he lifted a brow. "Afraid no one will hear you scream?"

Something like that, she thought, but when she saw the amusement in his dark gaze, she realized he was mocking her. Annoyance overcame her nerves. She pushed away from the fence. "What about your dog?"

"He's had his shots." Dillon opened the gate. Barking excitedly, the animal ran out.

"Yeah, but have you?" Rebecca approached cautiously. The dog sniffed at her shoes, looked up and barked once, then ran into the backyard.

"I only bite if you ask me nice," Dillon said when Rebecca moved past him through the gate.

Rebecca frowned at him. Yeah, right. Like *that* would ever happen.

The grass in the backyard was as neatly mowed

and edged as the front. A wrought iron table and chairs sat on a covered patio off a set of sliding glass doors. A split rail fence backed with wire enclosed a large vegetable and herb garden. Deep red tomatoes the size of softballs covered six tall bushes.

Rebecca remembered a movie she'd seen once called *The Last Supper.* It was about a group of friends who would invite a person to dinner, then during the course of the meal, vote whether the guest should live or die. The unlucky guests would be done away with, then buried in the garden under tomato plants, which proliferated in mutant proportions.

Hugging her purse close, Rebecca took some comfort in the knowledge she carried a container of Mace inside. When Dillon opened the side door to the garage, she hesitated once again.

He frowned. "If you've changed your mind—"

"No." She put her hand on the door when he started to close it. "I haven't."

She stepped inside. Dillon followed and flipped on a light, then closed the door.

Only one way in, Rebecca noted as she scanned the room. Only one way out.

The garage had been converted into a studio apartment. The walls were plastered white, the floor covered with dark blue commercial carpet. To Rebecca's right, a small wooden table and two chairs defined the kitchen's eating area. To her left, an open door revealed a bathroom with a shower. In the center of the apartment, a brown leather easy chair, reading lamp and coffee table made up the living room. In the far corner, a king-size bed shoved against the wall was obviously the bedroom. The scent of strong coffee hung heavy in the room.

Hardly the home of a man who was worth forty million dollars, Rebecca thought. But it was neat and clean and functional, and apparently, that was enough for Dillon.

She turned to face him, then gestured to the kitchen table. "May I?"

"Knock yourself out." He leaned against a kitchen counter. "Forgive me if I don't have tea and scones."

Or manners. She sat, then set her purse and the manila folder on the table. "Twenty-four years ago, your uncle Jonathan and aunt Norah were driving home from a long day at the Wolf River County Junior Rodeo and Fall Festival. Their three children, Rand, age nine, Seth, seven, and Elizabeth, almost three, were buckled in the back seat."

"Look, if you can't tell me something I don't already know, then this is—"

"Please, just let me start from the beginning and work my way through." She'd gone through it so many times in her head, she didn't know how else to do this. "Please."

Dillon clenched his jaw, then leaned against the doorjamb.

"A storm came up unexpectedly," Rebecca went on. "A flash of lightning in the middle of the road they were driving on caused the car to swerve and crash into a ravine. Jonathan and Norah were killed instantly."

Rebecca pulled the newspaper article from the file and set it on the table. Family Of Five Killed In Storm-Related Accident, the headline read. Dillon glanced at the article, then looked back at Rebecca.

"Your cousins didn't die that night, Dillon," Rebecca said quietly. "They were separated from each other and taken from the scene of the accident. Rand was told that his entire family had died and he was the sole survivor. Seth was told the same thing. Elizabeth was too little to understand anything that had happened. She didn't even know she'd been adopted until seven months ago."

"Adopted?" Dillon narrowed his eyes. "What do you mean, adopted?"

"They were all adopted. Rand, by an older couple in San Antonio. Seth, by a family in New Mexico. Elizabeth was sent to France, but her adopted parents, wealthy socialites from South Carolina, brought her back to the States a year later and told everyone she was their birth daughter."

"Becky," Dillon said impatiently, "you either haven't been taking your medication, or you need to up the dose. Even if a little bit of what you're saying were true and my cousins didn't die, how could they just disappear and be adopted out like that?"

"The adoptions weren't legal." Rebecca slipped a document from the folder and laid it beside the article. "A lawyer named Leon Waters made all the arrangements. A great deal of money exchanged hands between Waters and all the adoptive parents, all of it in cash."

"There had to be people at the crash site." Dillon shook his head in disbelief. "It's not possible that three children, all supposed to be dead, could be adopted out and no one would know."

"I didn't say no one knew."

He stared at her for a long moment. "Your mother?"

"She died eight months ago of lung cancer." Rebecca pulled a small leather-bound journal out of the folder and laid it on the table. "I found this in a lock box in her closet two months after her funeral. She wrote down everything that happened that night and the next three days. Every detail."

"You're telling me that your mother knew, and she said nothing?"

"More than that." Saying it out loud never got easier. If anything, it was more difficult. "She not only knew, she was a part of it."

"What do you mean, a part of it?"

"You said it yourself, Dillon." Rebecca closed her eyes. "Everything's about money. She was paid to take Rand away that night."

"Paid? Who paid her?"

Rebecca opened her eyes and met Dillon's hard gaze. "Your father."

Chapter 4

Y*our father.*

It took a moment for the words to sink in, and even when they did, Dillon couldn't quite get his brain around them. Neighborhood noise—the hum of an air conditioner from the house next door, the screech of a blue jay, the soft drone of a radio from the house next door. The beating of his heart. Every sound suddenly seemed amplified.

Your father.

"Miss Blake." He kept his voice even, and without blinking, met the deep green of her eyes. "That's a very serious accusation."

"It's not an accusation." She didn't look away. "It's a fact."

"Fact?" He snorted. "Because your mother scribbled something in a journal twenty-four years ago, does not make it fact. For all you know, she was writing a damn book."

"You want facts, here they are." Rebecca laid a fingertip on the newspaper article. "Fact. Your aunt and uncle had a car accident during a thunder storm and went into a ravine. Fact. Approximately ten minutes later, Sheriff Spencer Radick comes along, sees the headlights in the ravine and climbs down to see what happened. He finds Jonathan and Mary Blackhawk, in the front seat, both dead. Fact. Their three children are in the back seat, alive. Rand is unconscious, Seth is dazed, Elizabeth is whimpering."

"And you're saying the sheriff didn't call anyone for help?"

"He did call someone," Rebecca said. "He called your father."

"Why the hell would he do that?"

"William Blackhawk was one of the wealthiest and most powerful men in Wolf River County. He even had a seat on the city council. Everyone knew your father was estranged from both of his brothers, Jonathan and Thomas, because they'd married white women. If William saw either of them in town, or their families, he wouldn't even speak to them."

The truth of her statement rose like bile in Dillon's throat. Of course everyone in Wolf River knew that William Blackhawk hated his brothers, but no one would have dared say it out loud. Some things were only spoken in whispers and behind closed doors.

"It was common knowledge my father did not speak to my uncles," Dillon said dryly. "Which is exactly why it makes no sense that the sheriff would call him after the accident."

"According to my mother's journal, Spencer Radick was an ambitious man who had a serious gambling problem," Rebecca went on. "The sheriff saw an opportunity that night to pay off some of the debt choking him. Radick called your father, who arrived at the scene a few minutes later. Your father assessed the situation, made a decision and called my mother. He told her to leave me with the wife of one of the ranch hands, then meet him at the ravine, but told her not to tell anyone where she was going. Where she got there, he told her to take Rand to a hotel room in Dallas and he'd pay her very well to keep the truth quiet. Radick, who was single, took Seth home and your father took Elizabeth."

"Took her where?"

"To his lawyer, a man named Leon Waters."

Leon Waters. Dillon remembered the man. Medium height, with a thick chest and brown hair slicked back from a perpetually tanned, square face. Fancy suits and shiny shoes. On his pinkie finger, he always wore a large gold ring with a diamond the size of a dime. He came to the ranch on several occasions for business, had even stayed for dinner a few times. Dillon hadn't liked the lawyer, or the stench of whiskey on his breath when he'd leaned down and patted him on the head and told him he was a good kid.

But just because he hadn't liked the man didn't make him a criminal. Dillon shook his head. "My mother *never* would have allowed this."

"If she'd known, I'm sure she wouldn't have," Rebecca said, her voice softening. "According to my mother's journal, the only people who knew the truth were herself, Radick, Waters and your father."

"More speculation," Dillon said tightly. "How 'bout we get back to facts."

"Fine." Rebecca slid a piece of paper across the table. "This is an accident report filled out by Radick stating that your uncle Jonathan and all the passengers in his car were dead at the scene. There are also five reports from a hospital in Granite Ridge, detailing the injuries and confirming that each of the passengers in the car had died instantly. The medical examinations and hospital reports for Jonathan and Norah are accurate," Rebecca continued, "but Waters forged the other three and signed a different doctor's name, making it more difficult to trace. And who would question it, anyway? Outside of your family, the only living Blackhawk was Lucas, who was thirteen and living in a foster home at the time."

Lucas had lived in foster homes after both his parents died, Dillon knew, but the rest of Rebecca's story simply made no sense. It was as convoluted as it was insane. He'd have to be equally insane to believe a word she was telling him.

But that's what made it believable, Dillon realized. The fact that it was so incredible, so absolutely absurd, it just might be true.

"Why would my father go to all that trouble to make it look as if my cousins had died?" Dillon asked. "If he didn't want to raise the children himself, why didn't he just send them to a state facility?"

"Because if he split them up, adopted them out and had their names changed, they might not ever find out that he—with Leon Waters help—had altered your grandfather's will after he died. Land and holdings that your father knew were worth a fortune."

"Oh, for God's sake." With a dry laugh, Dillon

dropped his head back and stared at the ceiling. "Next thing you'll be telling me Father killed JFK and Marilyn Monroe, too."

"I realize I'm throwing a lot at you." Exhaustion crept into her voice. On a sigh, her shoulders slumped. "Dillon, believe me, I know what you're feeling right now. Exactly what I felt when I found this journal."

"You don't know crap about what I'm feeling, Miss Blake."

She stiffened, then, her back ramrod straight again, she slipped her purse over her shoulder and stood. "Just read the file and the journal," she said. "As I already told you, there's a phone number in the file for the lawyer in Wolf River handling this. He can verify everything I've told you."

He said nothing when she walked to the door and opened it. Bowie greeted her with a shrill bark and wagged his tail. She said something to the dog Dillon couldn't hear, and when she held out her hand, Bowie licked it.

Traitor.

"I'll be at the Mesa Motel until tomorrow morning." Rebecca rubbed Bowie's head. "You can call me there if you want to talk."

"And if I don't?"

She hesitated, held his gaze for a long moment, but didn't respond, just walked out the door and quietly closed it behind her. Dillon heard the squeak of the gate opening and closing, then the sound of her car starting and driving away.

He swore. One word, raw and crude, then dragged a hand over his face and struggled to rein in his emotions.

After he'd left Wolf River sixteen years ago, Dillon had been the proverbial loose cannon. He'd been seventeen, angry and looking for a fight. Because he was tall, most men had stayed out of his way. But eventually there would always be someone willing to oblige him. When fists flew, Dillon usually won, but win or lose, it never really mattered to him. All that had mattered—for a little while, at least—was that the lust for blood had been eased.

It had taken him a long time to cage that beast. And though it rattled its bars on occasion, he'd managed to keep the lock tightly secured.

Control was everything. It was the one thing he had, the only thing, that really meant something to him.

Except for the soft hum of the refrigerator, absolute silence closed around him like a fist. He stared at the leather journal, felt the icy chill slither up his neck.

If he opened that cage now, he wasn't sure he'd ever be able to close it again.

* * *

After a breakfast of orange juice and a packaged blueberry muffin from a vending machine at the gas station, Rebecca went back to the motel. While she watched a morning talk show with Regis Philbin and a rerun of *I Love Lucy,* she paced. She pulled out a paperback she'd bought at the airport and started on the plane, a compelling courtroom drama, but as interesting as the book was, she simply couldn't concentrate.

She waited, but he didn't call.

Sometime in the afternoon, she fell asleep, then took a quick shower to wake up. She left the bathroom door open in case the phone rang.

It didn't.

Frustrated and hungry, she gave up waiting and went in search of food that didn't require machines and quarters. One block from the motel, between Wilson's General Store and Hank's Hardware—If We Don't Have It, You Don't Need It—a neon pink flamingo sign lit the front window of Dina's Downtown Diner. The tantalizing scent of grilling hamburgers filled the early evening air and settled the decision where to eat dinner.

A bell tinkled overhead when she opened the door. Inside, chrome and pink vinyl were right out of the fifties. *Literally* out of the fifties, Rebecca thought, noting the sign on the cash register: Proudly Serving Resolute, Texas Since 1953.

A teenage boy and girl sat in a corner booth, but they were too busy making eyes at each other while they picked at a plate of French fries to notice her. At another booth, an elderly man working a crossword puzzle paid her no mind, either, but a younger man sitting at a table by the restrooms, a cowboy-type wearing a black Stetson, nodded politely when she closed the door behind her. An old jukebox that looked like the bumper and taillights from a pink '57 Chevy played doo-wop.

All I need is the poodle skirt, Rebecca thought, settling on a bar stool at the pink formica counter. She ordered an iced tea with extra lemon from a perky brunette waitress wearing—surprise—a pink uniform. While she waited for her tea, Rebecca reluctantly pulled out her cell phone and dialed, thankful that the music was loud enough to drown out any conversation she might have. She'd already put off making the call longer than she should have, and she knew there'd be hell to pay. "Thank you for calling West View Aviation. This is Desiree Lombardi speaking, General Manager. How may I help you?"

"General Manager are you?" Rebecca smiled at the familiar voice at the other end of the line. Desiree's Georgia drawl was as thick and sugary as winter molasses. "Last week you were Vice President of Operations. Don't tell me that my cheapskate brother finally gave you a promotion."

"*I* gave me a promotion," Desiree said with a throaty chuckle. "Now if only there was a raise to go along with it, I'd be happy as a pecan in caramel."

Rebecca laughed. With Desiree's light brown skin and bottle red hair, it seemed like a fitting description for the woman.

"Sugar, where *are* you?" Desiree scolded. "Sean's been downright ill-tempered for the past two days."

"How could you tell?" Rebecca teased.

"Rebecca." Desiree's scolding turned to worry. "You all right?"

"I'm fine, Des." Rebecca appreciated the woman's concern. Though Desiree was only a few years older, she had a mother-hen quality that made people feel warm and safe. "Is he there?"

"He's out in the hangar, sugar. Hang on while I page him."

Darn. One of the reasons Rebecca had waited so late to call was that she'd hoped her brother would either still be out on a charter or gone for the day. Apparently she hadn't been that lucky.

Story of my life at the moment, she thought with a sigh.

When the waitress slid a glass of iced tea and a plastic bowl of sliced lemon across the counter,

Rebecca smiled at the woman, then squeezed two wedges into her glass. Her smile faded when Sean's voice came on the line.

"Rebecca! For God's sake, where the hell have you been?"

"I told you I was signed up for a teaching seminar." It wasn't completely a lie. She *had* signed up for a teaching seminar. "Is there a problem?"

"You know damn well there's a problem," he snapped. "You haven't answered my last three messages."

"It's too loud, can't hear you," she said. In the background, the sound of a plane taking off made it almost impossible to hear. "Is that one of yours?"

"Yeah, hold on a second. Let me go back inside."

Though the scent of the grilling burgers had tempted her, Rebecca ended up ordering a chef's salad with ranch dressing while she waited for her brother to come back on the line. Over the past five years, Sean had slowly built up a private charter company that handled a lot of high-profile clients that included celebrities and wealthy business people from all over the world. He was handsome and single, but a workaholic. Rebecca wished he'd settle down and give her some nieces or nephews to play with and baby-sit, but the hours he kept considerably lowered the odds of him being grounded, so to speak, any time soon.

"All right, I'm here," Sean said a moment later and the background noise was now CB radio chatter. "Now where the hell are you?"

"I thought you were on a Canada run this week."

"I got back early, and stop trying to change the subject. Why haven't you returned my calls?"

"I'm calling you now." She kept her voice casual. "So what's up?"

"What's up? Melanie tried to call you at the hotel you were supposedly staying at for your supposed seminar, Rebecca. That's what's up."

Darn. With Melanie working on her latest sub-subatomic particle theory thesis at the family house in Nantucket and Sean gone most of the time, this should have been the best time to slip away for a few days unnoticed. For a moment, she considered dancing around the truth some more, but the fact was, she was so damn discouraged, she just didn't have it in her.

She took a long swallow of tea, hoping the cold caffeine would prep her for the impending lecture.

"I'm in Texas." The jukebox had switched from a quieter doo-wop to "Rock Around the Clock." When all she heard was silence at the other end of the phone, she bit her lip. "Sean?"

"Where?"

She heard the controlled fury in that single word. "Sean, I'm fine, and—"

"Where, dammit. I can be there in a couple of hours."

Sean's protectiveness had always been a blessing and a curse. He'd been twelve when his father married Rebecca's mother. Rebecca had been seven. It had never mattered to Sean that he didn't share genes with his stepsister. In Sean's eyes, and Rebecca's, they were blood. When baby Melanie came along one year later, with her big green eyes and mop of dark red hair, she solidified the blending of the two families.

They'd had it all. Money. Love. Prestige. Life had been perfect until Gregory Blake had unexpectedly died from a brain aneurysm three years ago. Still, the rest of the family had had each other to hold on to in their grief—until Rosemary Blake died two years after her husband.

And Rebecca found the journal.

Since that day, she'd had nothing to hold on to. The ground no longer felt solid under her. She'd had nothing she could trust. She'd even distanced herself from Sean and Melanie. For the first few months, they'd tried to give her some space, but lately, they'd been everywhere she turned, refusing to let her pull away. They didn't understand what she needed to do. What she *had* to do.

But then, she really didn't completely understand it herself. Didn't understand the driving desperation inside her to find Spencer Radick and Leon Waters. She simply knew she *had* to.

"Sean—" In spite of the loud music in the diner, Rebecca kept her voice low. "I found him."

There was a long pause. "Dillon Blackhawk?"

"Yes."

"Tell me where you are, Rebecca. We'll go together and speak to him. I can—"

"I already spoke to him." Rebecca could only imagine what Sean would do if he knew how Dillon had behaved. And she didn't want to imagine Sean and Dillon coming face-to-face. There was no question in her mind that fists would fly.

"Dammit, I told you if you found him that I'd go with you." Sean's voice rose. "You can't just approach some strange guy by yourself and tell him his father was a lying son-of-a-bitch."

"I was a little more diplomatic than that, for heaven's sake." Not that it had mattered, she thought. Any subtlety she'd managed had been wasted on Dillon Blackhawk. "Sean, I love you and Melanie, and I don't want to hurt either one of you, but you have to let me do this my way."

"Your way is too dangerous, Rebecca. You need backup. Melanie's worried sick." His voice softened. "I'm worried sick."

"I'm sorry," she whispered. "I'll call Melanie. And I'll check in with you more often. I promise."

"You really expect me to just sit around while you're off God knows where, doing God knows what? You're supposed to be the level-headed one in this family, Ree. This is crazy and you damn well know it."

Rebecca closed her eyes. Her head hurt. Not from the previous night's tequila anymore, but the entire situation. It would be so easy to give in to Sean's demands. So easy to lean on his strong shoulders the way she always had.

"Are you still there? Dammit, Rebecca, don't you hang up on me."

"I'm here," she said. "And stop yelling at me or I will hang up."

"Okay, okay, look." He sighed heavily. "At least tell me where you are and what happened."

"I'm in a little town called Resolute." When the waitress slid a plate of food across the counter, Rebecca's jaw went slack. The salad she ordered had to be the size of a basketball. Apparently, the everything's-bigger-in-Texas was no myth. "And nothing's happened yet. Dillon and I just talked this morning."

"You told him?"

"I told him."

"So how did he take it?"

Rebecca waited until the waitress moved away, then quietly said, "How would you take it? I'm giving him some time to absorb it all."

"Rebecca, I can fly in tonight," Sean said. "I promise I'll stay in the background."

"Sean, I'm sorry, but I can't." When the waitress came back with a rag and busily wiped at the already clean countertop, Rebecca realized she had an audience. "I've got to go. I'll call you in the morning."

Rebecca heard him swear under his breath, then sigh. It was easy to picture her brother dragging a frustrated hand through his short, dark hair while he shook his head.

"Call me tonight." It wasn't a request. "And Ree?"

"What?"

"Be careful."

"I will."

"I love you, sis."

"I love you, too."

Rebecca stared at the phone in her hand for a long moment after she hung up. She hated worrying her family, knew that if the situation were reversed, she'd be just as upset as Sean and Melanie. But she had to follow her heart this time. The only other person who could be on this path with her was the one person who didn't want to be.

"Boyfriend troubles?"

The waitress, who'd been eager to strike up a conversation, was now busy stuffing little packets of sugar into an already full little black plastic holder. Rebecca shook her head and slipped her phone into her purse. "Overprotective brother."

"I got me one of those. He's cute, but a pain in the butt." Sugar forgotten, the waitress wiped her palms on her apron, then stuck a hand out. "I'm Julie. You're that schoolteacher from Boston, aren't cha?"

Ah, small towns. Another blessing and curse. Rebecca shook her hand. "Rebecca Blake."

Julie glanced around the room, then folded her arms on the counter and leaned closer to Rebecca. "Charlene told me about you and Dillon Blackhawk."

Uh oh. Rebecca swallowed hard. "Charlene?"

"Charlene is Trudy's cousin, who's married to Charlie."

"Charlie?"

"You know, Dixie's brother." Julie lowered her voice. "Some say he's cheating on Trudy with a nurse who works at the clinic over in Yoakum. I say, what's he doing at the clinic in the first place, if you know what I mean."

Rebecca had no idea what Julie meant, but she gave the waitress a knowing nod anyway. Not even twenty-four hours had passed and it appeared that the phone lines were already burning up.

"It's a damn shame," Julie said with a sigh.

"Charlie and the nurse?" Rebecca asked cautiously.

"You and Dillon."

"Oh." Rebecca took a nervous sip of tea. "Right."

"So tell me." Julie leaned closer and arched one brow. "Is Dillon as hot in the sack as he is out of it?"

Rebecca choked. "Well, we never really, I mean, we weren't exactly—"

"It's okay, honey." Julie patted Rebecca's hand. "Trudy says no one's supposed to know. Don't you worry. Your secret's safe with me."

And Dixie and Trudy and Charlene and Charlie. Rebecca figured by noon that the rest of Resolute— all two thousand, three hundred and forty-five— would be included in her so-called secret.

Not sure what to say, Rebecca took a bite of sliced turkey. "Thanks."

"So is he?" Julie asked.

"Is he what?"

"Hot in the sack?"

"Oh." Rebecca saw the expectant look in the waitress's big brown eyes. She had to give the woman *something*. After all, she needed allies in this town, not enemies. Rebecca glanced to her left, then her right, then leaned in closer. "Let's just say you better keep the fire department on speed dial, if you know what I mean."

"No kidding," Julie said with a reverent whisper. "Damn."

Nodding, Rebecca stabbed a tomato. "And that's all I can say."

The bell over the door tinkled and a tall, lanky man wearing a blue gas company uniform walked in. He looked at Julie and grinned, then took a seat at the end of the counter.

Julie smiled back at the man, then sighed. "That's my boyfriend, Gil. He's a sweetie, but the only number we need on speed dial for him is the cable company. If he can't channel surf two thousand TV stations a night, he gets sore as a frog on a hot skillet."

Julie pushed away from the counter and picked up a coffeepot from the warming tray. Nothing like a boyfriend to cut short gossip regarding Dillon Blackhawk. "Me and Gil are meeting Dixie at the Backwater for happy hour tonight. Wanna join us?"

Rebecca had already had her year's quota of alcohol, but what the hell. Sitting in a bar with Julie and Gil and Dixie was better than sitting in a motel room staring at four walls. "Sure."

"Six o'clock," Julie said, then grinned. "Maybe you'll see Dillon there."

Not if he sees me first, Rebecca thought. "One can only hope."

Julie glanced at Gil and sighed again. "Ain't that the truth, honey."

Dillon stood in an alley across the street from the diner and watched Rebecca talking to the waitress at the counter. Julia, he thought the brunette's name was, but couldn't quite remember. She and her boyfriend were regulars at the Backwater Saloon, but other than a few games of pool with—what was his name…Bill?…no—Gil— Dillon couldn't say he really knew the couple. But then, other than Maria and Juan and Ilene, the nurse he'd taken out a couple of times, there were very few people in Resolute he actually knew beyond a first name basis.

Which was exactly the way he liked it.

Dillon knew people talked, but he'd never much cared one way or the other what people said about him. Gossip was like a sporting event, and in a small town, some folks trained for it like it was the Olympics. If you weren't a participant, then you became the event. Everyone knew everyone's business, and if they didn't, they made it up.

"About time," he muttered to himself when Rebecca finally came out of the diner. Though her stride carried purpose as she headed toward the motel, she didn't appear to be in a hurry. She had the body of a dancer, he thought. Loose-limbed, long legs, smooth lines. Her movements were graceful and measured, confident.

In spite of his annoyance with the woman, he couldn't help but be intrigued by her. She had the determination of a bulldog, but the face of an angel. One hell of a combination.

He'd gone for his run after Rebecca had left this morning. When he'd come back, he'd washed his truck, fixed a broken pipe in Maria's garden, then repaired a flat tire on Juan's bicycle. He'd done his best to avoid the folder Rebecca had left lying on the kitchen table. He saw no reason to read it, saw no reason to call the lawyer in Wolf River to verify Rebecca's story.

He already believed her.

Dillon knew his father had been an arrogant, ruthless man. A man capable of cruelty. But the thought of anyone splitting up a family—his own flesh and blood—then selling them off like cattle was inconceivable.

But that blood hadn't been pure. And Rebecca was right about William Blackhawk hating his own brothers for marrying white women. Before Dillon's grandfather passed away, William had tolerated an occasional family gathering with Jonathan and Thomas and their families. But after Red

Feathers' death when Dillon was eight, William had forbidden even the mention of Jonathan and Thomas in his house, insisting that his brothers had shamed and disgraced the Blackhawk name.

No one dared question William Blackhawk. He ruled his home, his family and his business with an iron fist. Swift retribution followed defiance of any kind. To this day, Dillon could still remember the sting of a slap across his face if he used the wrong tone.

Dillon could also remember the one and only time he'd struck back.

A quick honk of a horn pulled Dillon back to the present. Across the street, a red Mustang convertible pulled alongside Rebecca. Dixie Denison slid out of the driver's seat and ran over to Rebecca, gave her a hug, laughed about something, then jumped back into her car and drove off.

You've got to be kidding me.

Rebecca had barely been in Resolute twenty-four hours and already she was best friends with the mayor's niece.

Good God. Another twenty-four hours and the town would probably hold a parade and make Rebecca Grand Marshall.

Jaw clenched, Dillon watched Rebecca walk away. Enough was enough already. He needed to do something, and he needed to do it soon.

* * *

His day at the golf course had been a fruitful one, as well as pleasant. He'd shot a five under par, his best game ever, and that hot little cocktail waitress at the club—the one who not only had the best ass he'd ever seen, but the best pair of tits money could buy—had slipped him her phone number. 'Course, that was after he'd tipped her triple what he should have, but he figured a nice dinner and a few drinks and the broad would give him a lot more than her phone number.

But his day at the course had been promising on more than a personal level. The client he'd golfed with, Antonio Cabrini, was one of the wealthiest men in the world. Not that he was on any lists. Antonio's business was not one that was written about in *Forbes* or *Business Week.* No one, except Antonio himself, knew how much money he made, but it was enough to buy him anything in the world he wanted.

And he wanted a baby.

Actually, his wife wanted one. Antonio had three other children with his last two wives, but his current wife had suddenly been bitten by a maternal bug and decided she not only wanted one baby, she wanted two. Twins. A little boy and little girl. Wouldn't all her friends just be so envious?

Not that she would actually have them herself,

of course. She had a million-dollar body, one she had no intention of ruining with stretch marks or wasting months looking like a cow. She wanted two perfect babies, Italian, of course, like Antonio, and she wanted them now, before they left the States and went back to Naples.

Antonio called a friend, who called a friend. And there was only one name that came up, one man who could possibly fill such an order.

Leland Worthington.

Of all the names he'd taken over the years, Leland liked this one the best. It fit him, he thought. Had just a touch of the aristocratic, sounded as if he'd been born into nobility, instead of destitute field workers. From the time he was a child, he'd known he didn't belong in that world, that he was meant for bigger things. Money had been the only way out. He'd paid his own way through law school working insurance scams, set up his first practice as an estate attorney who knew how to work the client and the system. Leon Waters and Associates in Granite Springs had been a moderate success and he'd even made a decent income, but he'd still been a small fish until William Blackhawk had hired him. Other than the fact he'd been an Indian, William was everything Leon wanted to be. Rich, powerful, ruthless.

And now he—Leland Worthington—was just as

rich, just as powerful. Just as ruthless. That night twenty-four years ago had been a turning point for him. Who would have ever thought people would pay big bucks for a kid? Though ostensibly his practice was still financial and estate planning, he quietly made his real money in the baby business. Illegal adoptions. His clients never asked where he got the babies, and he never told. His nickname was The Stork, but he liked to think of himself more as Santa Claus. Spreading goodwill and cheer, bringing sunshine into people's lives.

The fact that he made a minimum of six figures per baby brought more than a little sunshine into Leland's life, too. Tax-free, untraceable, all deposited into a Swiss account.

He'd invested well, and his dream was finally coming true. If he could fill Antonio's order, the huge sum of money he'd make on the deal would simply be the icing on the cake before he left town in six days. It was a tough one, but he'd put the word out and see what came back.

When his cell phone rang, he was putting his clubs into the trunk of his silver Mercedes Roadster. He checked the caller ID and flipped open the phone.

"Well?"

"I found her," Edmunds said on the other line. "A little town called Resolute."

"And Dillon?"

"He lives here, but I don't know if she's talked with him yet."

Leland sighed. He'd had enough of this problem, had too many other things to think about. "Take care of them."

"Temporary, or permanent?"

Leland thought about it. Permanent was always better, but in this case, he'd be gone in a few days and it wouldn't matter what Dillon Blackhawk or Rebecca Blake did. And if they both died, there was always a possibility, though extremely remote, that their deaths might somehow trigger a more intense search.

"Put Dillon on the disabled list, then do whatever you want with the woman."

Leland snapped the phone shut. He knew exactly what Edmunds would do with the woman. But she'd brought it on herself, Leland thought and slammed his trunk shut. She should have stayed in Boston.

Soon, she'd wish she had.

Chapter 5

Rebecca dawdled in the dream. She lay on a smooth rock by a gentle stream, watching the sun sparkle off the clear water like diamonds on glass. A lush, green meadow surrounded her, the tall, slender reeds of grass bending softly in the cool breeze. Blue and yellow wildflowers dressed nature's canvas, scenting the air. Birds happily chirped from nearby trees.

Smiling, Rebecca stretched her legs and rolled to her side.

In the space of a heartbeat, the breeze turned cold and the birds fell silent. A shadow swept across the peaceful meadow, then a shrill screech of a bird sent a shiver rolling up her spine. She looked to the sky, saw the hawk circling overhead, its giant black wings spread wide, blocking out the sun. Claws and beak open, it dove straight for her.

Gasping, Rebecca opened her eyes.

A dream. Just a dream, she told herself. She closed her eyes again and shivered, waited for her pulse to calm down while the pieces of reality dropped into place.

Hotel room. Resolute. Sunday.

Dillon Blackhawk.

Well it certainly didn't take a genius to figure out *that* dream.

Pulling the blanket tighter, she shivered again, wished she'd had on something heavier than the thin cotton tank top and boxers she'd worn to bed. Why was it so cold in the room? she wondered. And so dark. Blinking away the haze still fogging her eyes, she glanced at the bedside clock and with a soft groan, realized it was barely six o'clock. Darn. She'd been so tired when she'd come in at one o'clock this morning, Rebecca had thought she'd sleep at least until late morning. Instead, thanks to Dillon Blackhawk invading her dream, she'd managed only five hours.

She hadn't intended to stay out so late last night, but she'd actually had a nice time with her new acquaintances. She'd played several games of nine ball with Dixie and darts with Julie, then Gil had entertained her with stories about the trials and tribulations of reading gas meters in rural-town America. They'd teased her about drinking nothing more than soda all evening, but hadn't really pushed the issue. Gil had been a perfect gentleman, and he'd even called his brother, Mike, to come join them.

Rebecca had suspected there had been some matchmaking going on, especially when Julie insisted that Mike play a game of pool with Rebecca, then sit next to her at the table. But even though Gil's brother had been a nice enough guy, and had even borne a slight resemblance to Brad Pitt, the last thing in the world Rebecca had time for right now was a man.

Except Dillon, of course, though she certainly wasn't interested in him in a romantic sense. He was the opposite of any man she'd ever dated, though if she were to be honest, she'd only dated a few men. In her junior year of college, she'd gone out with Darrin, a friend of Sean's, but they'd ended up being better friends than lovers. Then she'd met Matt, a financial planner, at one of her mother's charity fund-raisers, but he'd had more of a relationship with his stocks and bonds than he'd had with her. She'd also briefly dated one of the other teachers at school, but that had ended with all the gusto of a Fourth of July fireworks dud.

She wanted to meet Mr. Right, wanted to feel that *zing* in her heart and that flutter in her stomach whenever he walked into the room. She wanted to bounce babies on her hip, tickle their soft tummies and hear them laugh. She wanted a house outside of the city, to know her next door neighbor's name. Barbecue steaks on a backyard grill. In a year or two, she'd be ready for all that. But not now.

Now, if she wanted a future, she had to deal with the past.

At the moment, though, her immediate concern was the fact that she was freezing. Hugging her arms tightly around her, she slipped out from under the warmth of her covers and ran to the air conditioner, then quickly flipped it from High to Off. Teeth chattering, she hurried back to bed and jumped back under the covers. Funny, but she could have sworn she'd set the control to low last night. Apparently, she didn't know what she was doing these days.

Wide awake now, she stretched again, then decided she might as well shower and get dressed rather then lay here in the semidark, thinking about her limited history of dating and her plans for a husband and children. She started to slip out of bed again and froze.

She saw the silhouette of a large man sitting in the corner. Her heart slammed against her ribs and she forced back a scream. Adrenaline pumped through her veins, had her gripping the edge of the blanket. But she knew if she tried to run to the door, she'd never make it in time. If she screamed, the man could be on top of her in a split second.

Calm, she told herself. *Stay calm.*

Her pepper spray was in her purse on the nightstand, but she knew the odds of reaching the canister before the man could stop her was very slim. Still, as weak as the plan was, it was the only one she had.

Heart pounding furiously, she slipped back under the covers and inched her way across the mattress.

"Mornin,' Becky."

At the sound of the all-too familiar voice, she went absolutely still. It took a moment to find her voice, and even when she did, the name emerged as a raspy whisper. "Dillon?"

"You expecting anyone else?"

Narrowing her eyes, she blinked, tried to make out his face, but there still wasn't enough light coming in through the drawn drapes. Relief, profound and intense, poured through her veins, only to be quickly replaced by sharp, hot anger.

"What the *hell* are you doing in my room?"

"You wanted to talk," he said as casually as if they were sitting on a porch swing. "Here I am."

You wanted to talk? Here I am? Hysteria hovered, and she put a hand at the base of her throat to calm herself. "I had the deadbolt and chain on that door. How did you get in here?"

"That's not really important."

"It most certainly is." She wanted to make sure it would never happen again.

"Did you have a good time last night with Dixie and her friends?"

Apparently, he wasn't going to answer her question. She wished she could see his face, but the best she could make out was the slash of his dark brows and his long hair brushing the tops of his broad shoulders. "You broke into my room and scared me half to death to ask me if I had a good time last night?"

"Are you scared of me, Becky?"

"I'm not Becky anymore." Not even her mother had called her that since the night they'd left the Circle B. A new life, her mother had told her. An adventure. "And no, I'm not scared of you."

"Liar." He stood. "I can hear it in your voice."

Rebecca swallowed hard. In the darkness, Dillon appeared even taller, his chest wider, his shoulders bigger. So maybe she *was* a little frightened.

Maybe even a lot. But she sure as hell wasn't going to let him know that.

"I wake up and there's a strange man in my room." She pulled the blanket closer when he moved toward the bed. She'd inched over enough that her purse was within an arm's length of her now. If she had to, she'd use the spray on him. "I'd be stupid not to be scared."

"And you're not stupid, are you?" He stopped at the foot of the bed. "In fact, you're quite smart. You graduated cum laude from Brown, wrote your thesis on 'The Effects of Advanced Socio-Economic Principals on the Educational Standards of Inner-City Schools,' then worked for two years in the educational research department before you took a position teaching third graders in an underprivileged school, which is where you've been for the past three years."

Rebecca's jaw went slack. "How did you—how do you know that?"

"You aren't the only one who has access to information," he said matter-of-factly. "I also know that even though you work in one of the poorest areas of Boston, you live in one of the wealthiest. Your mother divorced your biological father in Ireland when you were three, came to the States when you were four, then married Gregory Blake the Third when you were seven. You have an older stepbrother named Sean who owns a private charter airplane company and a sister named Melanie who's studying for her doctorate in physics at the ripe old age of twenty-four. You also took piano lessons for eight years, but according to your teacher, you were never very good at it."

Dillon took tremendous pleasure in watching Rebecca's mouth drop open and her eyes widen. He'd slipped into her room just under an hour ago and watched her sleep while he'd waited for the dawn.

No one had seen him come in, just as no one would see him leave.

"How could you *possibly* know any of that?" she asked, her tone incredulous.

"Like I said—" he shrugged "—you aren't the only one who knows how to dig around a person's past. So how's it feel now that the shoe's on the other foot, sweetheart?"

Her mouth snapped shut, and she lifted her chin. "There was no other way to find you. Like *I* said before, you didn't make it easy."

"That should have been a hint," he said dryly. "If I left here today, trust me, I can make sure you won't find me again."

His threat seemed to take the wind out of her sails. Her shoulders sagged, then she lifted her knees and dropped her forehead down on them.

"Please don't," she whispered. "Please don't leave."

The utter desperation in her voice surprised Dillon, but not nearly as much as the hitch in his chest at her soft plea. He told himself to walk away now and not look back, knew that it would be a mistake to continue this conversation, especially considering the fact that Rebecca was half-naked under the covers she'd clutched to her chest.

He had no trouble admitting that he was physically attracted to the woman. He might resent her sudden and unwanted appearance in his life, but he'd have to have ice water in his veins not to appreciate her female qualities. After sitting here for the past hour watching her sleep, listening to her soft sighs, he couldn't stop himself from wondering what it would feel like to join her in that big bed. Wondering how her breasts would fit in the palms of his hands. If she would taste as good as she smelled. If she had the same determination and spirit in bed as she did out of it?

He'd finally turned the air conditioner up full blast, not only to wake her, but to cool the burn in his blood. When she'd ran to the air conditioner to turn it down, he'd caught a glimpse of smooth, creamy white thighs and firm, unfettered breasts. He was damn glad it was dark in the room, or he'd have greeted Rebecca with a lot more than a simple good morning.

But the distress in her voice and the slump of her lovely shoulders cooled his desire more than the blast of icy air. He swore silently. "What do you want from me?" Lifting her head, she dragged both hands through her hair. "What my mother and your father did was deplorable."

"I'm not responsible for my father's sins, Rebecca." Lord knew he had enough of his own. "Nor are you responsible for anything your mother did."

"It's not about accepting responsibility." She wrapped her arms around her knees. "It's about setting things right."

"They're both dead." He didn't like the direction this conversation was going, didn't like what he thought she was suggesting. "A little late for retribution."

"Radick and Waters are still out there somewhere."

"Or maybe they're both dead, too."

"Maybe they are," she acknowledged. "But I have to know."

"Why do you have to know?" He paced to the corner and turned back again. "You can't change a damn thing that happened twenty-four years ago. My cousins are reunited and they have their inheritance. That should be enough."

"It's not." She shook her head. "What if Waters is still buying and selling children?"

"Bad things happen to good people. You can't save them all."

"Nobody knows that better than me," she said softly. "But if we found Waters, and if we could help even one person whose life he's ruined, then maybe, just maybe, that would set the past right."

"Nothing—and no one—can set the past right." He shook his head. "Not you, and certainly not me."

"We can," she insisted. "If we can find Radick, then I'm certain we can find Waters and—"

"Don't you get it, there is no *we*." He stepped to the side of the bed and reached for her shoulders, heard her gasp when he lifted her to her knees and pulled her close. "This is as close to *we* as it gets."

He dropped his mouth down on hers, his intention solely to intimidate. Whatever it took to send her packing. She might not realize it, he told himself, but he was doing her a big favor. When she gasped, he parted her lips with his tongue and plundered, waited for her to pull away, waited for her to strike him and call him a bastard.

When she did none of those things, just held very still in his hands, neither moving away or leaning closer, he knew he'd made a serious tactical error.

Anger and surprise had him yanking his mouth

away from hers. He swore, told himself to let go, but the need, the desire, was already raging through him and there was nothing he could do. His mouth came down a second time.

This time, not to punish or frighten, but to pleasure.

Her hands lightly touched his arms, whether to steady herself or explore he didn't know. But he did know that her soft fingers on his skin was like kindling to the fire racing through his veins. He slid an arm around her back and dragged her against him, felt the wild beating of her heart. Or was it his? Heard the sound of her ragged breath mingling with his. Two thin layers of cotton separated bare skin from bare skin. Her breasts molded to him. Soft. Yielding. The feel of her hardened nipples against his chest shattered the voice inside his head telling him to stop this insanity before it got out of hand.

Who the hell was he kidding? It was already out of hand.

From the second his mouth had touched hers, hell, probably from the moment he'd first laid eyes on her, he'd felt the hunger for her. An intense, almost primitive need to touch, to taste. To own.

The thought startled him, had him jerking back. He released her, then stepped away. They were both breathing hard, and the sound echoed in the room. Early morning light had slipped through the top of the window drapes, enough for Dillon to see the stunned embarrassment on Rebecca's face, enough for him to see her lips were swollen and damp from his kiss.

He closed his hands into fists to keep from reaching for her again.

"Like I said, there is no *we*," he said through clenched teeth. "Go home, Rebecca."

"I can't." She sank to her knees. "I have to find them, Dillon. With or without you."

He wanted to shake her, was afraid if he did that he'd only end up kissing her again. *Damn fool woman!*

"You think you can just walk up to Radick or Waters and tell them they've been naughty boys? You think they'll fall at your feet and beg forgiveness?" Frustration seared him to the bone. "Men like Radick and Waters will tear your heart out and dice it up without so much as a blink of an eye."

"I'll take my chances." She held her gaze steady with his. "I told you, I'm not stupid."

"I'm beginning to change my mind on that." He stared at her for a long moment, then said more quietly, "Go home now, Rebecca, or you'll end up in a body bag."

Without looking back, he strode across the room and opened the door. When she called to him, he stopped at the door and glanced over his shoulder.

"Just for the record," she said. "I was a damn good pianist."

Under different circumstances, he might have smiled. But under different circumstances, he realized, he wouldn't be here at all.

Turning, he opened the door and quietly slipped out of her room.

It took Rebecca a full ten minutes to stop shaking, another ten minutes after that before she felt her legs would be strong enough to hold her up. Her senses were still reeling when she finally stood beside the bed, in the very spot where Dillon had stood. A shudder ran through her.

He kissed me.

I kissed him back.

On a groan, she closed her eyes. How could that possibly have happened? For a moment, she even questioned *if* it had happened. In the stillness of her room, the quiet, the line between dream and reality seemed blurred. She touched her fingers to her mouth. Oh, it had happened, all right, she thought. Her lips still tingled. For that matter, her whole body tingled.

She could still feel his large hands on her shoulders, could still feel the power and strength in his grip when he'd lifted her up from the bed. Could still feel his mouth on hers.

Good God. She hadn't discouraged him in the slightest. If anything, she'd welcomed him. She'd *wanted* his mouth on hers, his hands on her. Had wanted her hands on him. Logic dictated that Dillon had simply taken advantage of her exhaustion and her emotional state.

It was the *situation,* she told herself, the need to connect to another human being. In a moment of extreme vulnerability, she'd been caught off guard.

But it was more than that, she knew. So much more than loneliness, or fear or fatigue. It went deeper, was definitely more profound. No one had ever made her feel like that before. His kiss had rocked her to the core.

Though it hardly made her feel safe, Rebecca chained the door and set the deadbolt again, even locked the bathroom door while she showered, for all the good it would do. She doubted a simple lock would slow the man down if he decided to come back.

She still had no idea how he'd gotten into her room so easily and so quietly, but it had certainly been a lesson to her on safety. From now on, she'd put a chair in front of the door and keep her Mace within an arm's length.

Not that she was really worried about Dillon returning. He'd made it perfectly clear he wouldn't help her. As disappointed as she was, she knew she had no choice but to accept his decision. She certainly couldn't force him to help her. She doubted anyone could force Dillon Blackhawk to do anything he didn't want to do.

Maybe he was right, she thought while she quickly toweled off, then pulled on a pair of jeans and white sleeveless blouse. Maybe she *was* stupid. Just because their paths had crossed twenty-four years ago certainly didn't bond them in any way. Sean had always told her she was too much of an idealist, that a little cynicism was a healthy thing. Until today, she hadn't believed him. But now she realized how foolish she'd been to hope that Dillon would share her feelings on righting the wrongs that had been committed.

She tucked her toiletry bag into her suitcase and zipped it closed, wondered if the man had any feelings at all.

Rebecca looked at the rumpled sheets on the bed, couldn't stop the shiver that ran through her. With a sigh, she stepped out into the early morning light, then drew in the scent of bacon frying that drifted on the already warm air. She needed coffee and food before she hit the highway. Not that she even knew where she was going, but she grabbed a map out of the glove box, anyway, then headed for the diner.

The restaurant was busy and every seat at the counter was already occupied. Rebecca settled into a window booth and ordered coffee and a scrambled eggs special from a slow-moving, sleepy-eyed platinum blonde. There wasn't one familiar face in the diner this morning, but based on the curious looks coming from the other patrons, Rebecca figured everyone in the place knew who she was.

What did it matter if they stared? she thought, opening her map. After she finished her meal, checked out of the motel and gassed up her car, Resolute would be a tiny speck in her rear view mirror. And though she'd given her home phone number and address to Dixie and Julie and told them to visit if they were ever in Boston, Rebecca didn't really expect to hear from the women. In a strange way, she'd miss them. Without a doubt, they had been two of the more colorful people she'd met in her life.

She was on her second cup of coffee and picking at a mountain of scrambled eggs and diced ham when she noticed a man wearing a tan sheriff's uniform enter the diner. He had the face of a bloodhound, but the body of a pit bull—small and compact, solid. He wore a white cowboy hat over short gray hair. His expression was somber as he spoke with the waitress, then he glanced across the restaurant at Rebecca.

Terrific. When she hadn't left town quickly enough, Dillon had probably sent the law to give her a boot in the butt. She watched the sheriff approach, then stop beside her table.

"Rebecca Blake?"

"Yes?"

"Sorry to bother you while you're eating." He rested one hand on his gun, the other on a pair of handcuffs. "I'm Sheriff Keber."

She wasn't certain if she was supposed to congratulate the man or hold out her wrists. "What can I do for you, Sheriff?"

"My daughter Julie works here at the diner," he said. "She tells me you're a close friend of Dillon Blackhawk's."

Close friend? Rebecca almost laughed at the absurdity of the sheriff's comment. "We know each other."

"Would you mind coming with me?"

Even for Dillon, this was going too far, Rebecca thought angrily. Though her insides were shaking with fury, she calmly picked up her coffee cup and sipped. "Come with you where, Sheriff?"

"To the hospital," Keber said. "Seems that your boyfriend's been in an accident."

Chapter 6

Rebecca sat in the empty waiting room at Resolute Memorial. The one-story brick and glass building on the edge of town appeared to be more of an urgent-care clinic than an actual hospital. The pale blue tiled floor was shiny clean, the off-white walls freshly painted. A tall, artificial palm tree graced one corner, and a brightly lit rectangular fish tank stood in the other. The hospital receptionist, a gray-haired woman with bifocals, had offered coffee or tea, but Rebecca had politely declined and the woman had turned back to the movie she'd been watching on the television mounted outside the registration desk.

Other than Dillon, it appeared that the hospital was having a slow morning.

Rebecca had no idea what the extent of Dillon's injuries were. All she knew was that his truck had gone off a road and hit a tree. And though she doubted that Dillon would appreciate her concern, she'd come anyway. As much as she hated to admit it, she was worried about him.

It was strange, the connection she felt with Dillon. It went deeper than their past, and beyond her own need to seek retribution for her mother's transgressions. Whatever it was, she simply couldn't walk away knowing he'd been hurt.

Rebecca glanced at the clock on the waiting room wall. It had been ten minutes since the sheriff had gone to check on Dillon, but it felt more like ten hours. She tried to watch the movie on the television, an old musical with Fred Astaire and Ginger Rogers, but she just couldn't concentrate. Picking up a women's health magazine on an end table, she quickly flipped through the pages, then dropped it back down again.

What could possibly be taking so long? Unless Dillon's injuries were serious, she thought, chewing on a fingernail. So serious that they were working on him now, like an episode of ER, with a team of doctors and nurses rushing around yelling unintelligible medical procedures.

She shook her head at her own ridiculous imagination, but still, the image had her out of her chair and heading for the receptionist. Before she reached the woman, Sheriff Keber pushed open the double doors.

"You can come back now, Miss Blake."

Finally.

Clutching her purse, Rebecca followed the sheriff through the doors, then walked past a nurse's station where a pretty blonde was filling out a chart. A shiny metal name badge identified her as Ilene Baker, R.N. *Ilene Baker.* Dixie and Jennie had told Rebecca that Dillon had dated the woman.

Rebecca expected the nurse to glare at her as she walked by the station, but when the blonde glanced up, she merely smiled.

"He's in room six." The nurse pointed down the hall. "Third door on the right. Doc's with him now."

"I have to leave, but you go on ahead," Sheriff Keber said to Rebecca. "If you need a ride back to the motel, I can have the manager come get you."

"Thank you, but it's not that far. I can walk back."

"A city gal that walks. Fancy that." Smiling, he looked at Ilene. "Better get a room ready. I just got a family disturbance call."

"Edith and Hank?" the nurse asked.

"Yep. I'm not sure if Hank's getting slower or Edith's aim is getting better, but if she's conked that husband of hers with a frying pan again, the doc'll have to check him out. I should put her in a cell this time, though if I tried, she'd probably conk me, too. Miss Blake—" the sheriff looked at Rebecca and smiled "—been a real pleasure."

The sheriff strolled away through the double doors. Not certain what to do, Rebecca shifted awkwardly, then looked at Nurse Baker. "Should I wait until the doctor is finished?"

The blonde shook her head. "No need. He could probably use your help."

My help? Rebecca frowned at the nurse's comment, but decided not to question it. Turning, she moved down the small corridor. Though the hallways of Resolute Memorial were nothing at all like Massachusetts General, the smell and feel of the sterile environment was all too familiar to her.

This was the first time Rebecca had been in a hospital since her mother had passed away. Emotions, raw and tender, rose up and threatened to overwhelm her, but she pushed them aside, tucked them back into that place where she still privately grieved. This was not the place, and definitely not the time, to let her feelings have control.

Rebecca stopped just outside room six, heard the sound of male voices inside. The door was halfway open, but a closed curtain hid the bed from her view. She knocked lightly on the door.

The curtain slid aside and a short, plump man with bulldog cheeks stuck his head out. He held a tiny flashlight in one hand. "Ah, you must be Miss Blake. Just in time." The doctor slipped the flashlight into a top pocket on his white coat. "I was about to order a crankectomy."

Rebecca glanced at Dillon. Frowning at the doctor, Dillon lay on the bed, arms crossed tightly over the hospital gown he wore. Rebecca's heart jumped at the two-inch line of neat stitches over his left eyebrow. A purple and blue discoloration spread across the swollen eyelid.

"A crankectomy?" she asked hesitantly.

"It's a procedure to treat IPS, otherwise known as Irritable Patient Syndrome." The doctor offered his hand. "Dr. Edward Thompson."

Trying not to smile, Rebecca shook Dr. Thompson's smooth hand. "A pleasure."

"If you two are done having a laugh at my expense," Dillon grumbled, "I'd like to get the hell out of here."

Dr. Thompson sighed and turned back to his patient. "Your X rays aren't back, and even if they were, I wouldn't release you just yet. I suggest you relax and enjoy the company of a pretty lady."

Dillon's frown turned to a scowl. "A scratch and a few bruises is no reason to keep me here, Doc. You've already stitched me up. If the X rays show a problem, I'll come back. I want my clothes, dammit."

"If you'd like to walk home wearing your boots and a hospital gown, you're welcome to leave," Dr. Thompson said patiently. "Otherwise, you'll wait."

When Dillon simply glared, the doctor gave Rebecca a look of condolence. "If you'll excuse me, I'll go check on those X rays."

Shaking his head, Dr. Thompson left the room. Rebecca bit the inside of her lip and took a cautious step forward. "How are you?"

"Terrific." Dillon laid his head back on the pillow and stared at the ceiling. "My truck went one-on-one with a tree. Apparently, the tree won."

Rebecca decided it was a good sign that Dillon hadn't lost his sarcasm. If he'd been anything but irritable and terse, she would have been much more concerned. "What happened?"

"Some idiot in a blue pickup tried to pass me and clipped my rear bumper instead." He grimaced when he shifted his weight. "Next thing I knew, I was in the back of an ambulance on my way here. The son of a bitch didn't even hang around."

Rebecca moved beside the bed. Dillon looked like a boxer at the end of a ten-round fight. Between the stitches and the swelling around his left eye, he had to be hurting. Not that the man would ever admit it, she thought. Dillon Blackhawk was too proud, too stubborn and definitely too macho for his own good.

He glanced up, focused his blurry gaze on her. "What are you doing here?"

"I was packed and ready to leave," she said. "But the sheriff found me at the diner and told me you had an accident. I just wanted to make sure you were all right. See if there's anything you need."

She was the last person Dillon would have expected to see at his bedside. After the way he'd treated her, after he'd refused to help her. After he'd kissed her and coldly walked away. Most women would have been so damn mad, they would have celebrated his accident.

But then, he already knew that Rebecca wasn't most women.

"What I need," he said quietly, "is for you to give up this crazy quest of yours." There was no heat in his words, no annoyance, and it surprised even him. "Go back to Boston and let the past be."

It seemed as if she were actually considering his suggestion. The fatigue and discouragement in her eyes was evident. The unexpected, and unwelcome, desire to touch her, to soothe away that fatigue, surprised him. Maybe he couldn't stop her, but he sure as hell wouldn't help her, either. The best case scenario was that she'd run around Texas looking for her needle in a haystack, then finally go home.

He didn't want to think about the worst case scenario.

There was a knock at the door, then Sheriff Keber walked back into the room and looked at Dillon. "I just got a call from Walt that you might be interested in. Looks like he found the truck that hit you. Blue, right front bumper dented. It was hidden off the highway on the edge of town, behind a stand of trees. Belongs to Arnie Howard."

Dillon knew Arnie from the Backwater Saloon. He was a local ranch hand whose wife had kicked him out of the house because he drank too much. Dillon had never paid the cowboy any mind, but he sure as hell would now. He tossed the covers off, ignored the pain that shot from his jaw to the temple. "Where the hell is he?"

"In Houston." Sheriff Keber's circle of keys clinked when he looped his thumbs around his belt. "Walt called Arnie's mom when he found the truck. She says Arnie and Josh Merino are competing in a bull riding championship and been gone five days."

Five days? Dillon narrowed his eyes. "So who was driving his truck?"

"Can't say just yet. But according to June—" the sheriff looked at Rebecca "—that's Arnie's mom, Arnie parked his truck behind the Citco and left it there. Anyone could have decided to take it for a drive, then got scared after they hit you and dumped it behind those trees. My money it was one of Eli Haber's teenagers, or all of them. They aren't really bad kids, but with school out, they got too much time on their hands. Arnie's truck sitting all by itself, with him gone, is like a neon sign over a whore house offering free samples." Sheriff Keber took off his hat and slid Rebecca an apologetic look. "Pardon me, Miss Blake."

Rebecca smiled. "No problem."

"Anyway—" the sheriff looked at Dillon "—Walt's having Arnie's truck towed to the body shop. I gotta handle a domestic dispute, then I'll go check it out and get back to you. I reckon we'll find out who the guilty party is soon enough. Pretty hard to hide anything in this town."

That was like saying cows had cud, Dillon thought irritably, watched the sheriff slip his hat back on and touch the brim. "Miss Blake. Dillon."

Dillon stared at the doorway after the sheriff left. Whoever had gone for a joy ride in Arnie's truck wasn't too bright, and they sure as hell couldn't drive worth a damn, either. Which meant they were either drunk, or never drove a truck before. Whatever the case, Dillon would know soon enough who was responsible. Then there would be hell to pay.

"Dillon." Rebecca's voice cut into his thoughts

of revenge. He slid his gaze from the doorway and looked at her. "I—I'm going now," she said. "I'm sorry about your truck and for any trouble I've caused you. I realize the accident probably wouldn't have happened if you hadn't come to see me this morning."

That was probably true, he thought, but irrelevant. When he said nothing, she hesitated, then lifted her hand, as if to reach out to him. He stiffened, afraid if she touched him, if she asked him one more time for his help, he just might change his mind.

To his relief, she dropped her hand, then gripped the straps of her purse and backed toward the door. "I'm sorry," she said again, then turned and left.

Slowly, he released the breath he'd been holding.

It shouldn't matter to him one way or the other, but he hoped she would come to her senses. Hoped she would realize that even if he had helped, their odds of success would have been slim. Hoped she realized that without him, she didn't have a snowball's chance in hell.

Closing his eyes, he laid his head back against the pillow. He didn't want to think about Rebecca anymore. Didn't want to think about why she'd come here. How soft her lips had felt under his. Didn't want to think about the accident, or what his truck looked like after kissing a tree.

He didn't want to think, period.

The medication they'd given him earlier had dulled the pain in his head and his knee, but did nothing for the sharp sense of uneasiness looming over him. It was like a hand on the back of his neck, not quite touching, but he could feel the heat rippling along his shoulders. It was only a feeling, but he couldn't shake it.

He rubbed at his chest, then winced at the bruise under his hand. He wasn't sure what he'd hit his head on, but he could still feel the slam of his upper body against the steering wheel, and the impact of his knee against the console. And then he'd blacked out.

And though he didn't want to think, he knew he had to try and make sense of what had happened. Knew there would be no peace until he did. He retraced his steps....

He'd left Rebecca at the motel, had driven side streets for a little while, then turned onto the highway. The road ahead of him and behind had been empty. Normal for an early Sunday morning. His window had been rolled down and he'd rested his arm on the door. The light was still gray, the air quiet. Very quiet.

His thoughts had wandered. He couldn't get Rebecca off his mind. He'd been frustrated, sexually and mentally, and he'd been angry that she was so damn stubborn. He remembered he'd been arguing with himself whether he should go back and argue with her again, or go back and kiss her again. He'd wanted to do both.

He still did.

Pushing that thought away, Dillon opened his eyes and stared at the ceiling. Whatever had happened, he hadn't been paying attention. He'd looked up into his rearview mirror only a split second before the truck clipped him.

A split second.

He closed his eyes again, forced his emotions aside, forced his mind to slow down so he could retrace that moment. The blue truck. A single driver. A man. Both hands on the wheel, looking directly at him.

Dillon's eyes flew open.

Son of a bitch.

Teresa slowly climbed the flight of stairs to her second-story room at the Crescent Hotel. On the bottom level, a young woman in a very tight, short skirt and low cut blouse was opening a door for a man in a suit, who glanced nervously both ways before disappearing inside the room with the woman. At the top of the stairs, wearing T-shirts and oversized pants, two teenagers with tattoos passed a beer can back and forth while they smoked cigarettes.

They'd been there yesterday, too, when Teresa had checked into the shabby hotel. She had the feeling they were lookouts for a room to the left, number 18. She had no idea what went on in that room, and she didn't want to know. Right now, all she wanted was to be alone.

The teenagers looked at her, but thankfully, the sight of an extremely pregnant woman was not one to illicit cat calls or crude remarks. Her pulse pounded with fear, but she kept her gaze down and passed by the young men, holding her breath so she wouldn't breathe in their cigarette smoke. They let her pass, but even as she turned to the right and headed for her room at the end of the corridor, she could feel their leery eyes on her.

She felt sick to her stomach.

Inside her room, she ran to the bathroom and threw up, then sat on the tile floor until the spasms passed. She managed to pull herself up and rinse out her mouth, then ran a thin, dingy washcloth under cold water and wiped her face.

I'm so sorry, Miss Bellochio. As of last Friday, Mr. Gavin is no longer employed here. If he hired you, there's no record of it.

Teresa still felt numb. When she'd spoken to the man at the insurance company only four days ago, he'd not only assured her he had a job for her in his office, but he'd even promised her an advance on her first paycheck. Now it was as if the man didn't exist. She'd come all the way here for nothing. With nothing. The little bit of money she had might pay for food and three or four nights at this horrible excuse for a hotel, but then she'd have nothing.

A sharp tug across her belly made her suck in a breath. The twinges were getting stronger, and seemed to be coming more often, though not with any pattern. Braxton Hicks, she told herself, then closed the lid on the toilet and sat. False labor pains were normal, she assured herself again. And right now, a few erratic contractions were hardly her biggest problem. It was finding a job.

Who would hire an eight-month pregnant woman? When she'd explained her situation to Mr. Gavin, he'd been so kind, so helpful, had told her she could bring her baby to work with her, that the company had a child care program. It had been perfect. A dream come true.

A dream that had turned into a nightmare.

She closed her eyes to hold back the burn of tears, then laid her forehead on the counter. Teresa thought about calling her parents, but didn't think she could bear it if they hung up on her again. She was so tired. And scared. Not for herself, but for her baby.

When another sharp contraction made her gasp,

she wrapped her arms around her belly. *It's too soon*, she told herself. She *couldn't* be in labor yet.

Oh, dear God, but what if she was?

When the contraction finally passed, Teresa washed her face again and picked up her purse. The thought of bringing her baby into the world in this seedy hotel was too horrible to bear. She couldn't take a chance, wouldn't risk her baby's health. She'd passed a clinic two blocks from the hotel. Surely someone there would help her. There were good people in this world.

No matter what had happened, she still believed that with all her heart.

Rebecca walked past St. Mary's Presbyterian Church and heard the sound of joyful singing. The little white steepled church was a block from Main Street on the edge of town and the graveled parking lot was full of cars and trucks. She paused to listen, recognized the song she'd sang herself many times on Sunday mornings. Growing up, church had been mandatory for the Blake family, and though she'd complained about it many times, Rebecca realized how much she missed those Sunday mornings. Missed the people and the songs and feeling of love.

When this was over, she would start going to services again, she told herself. When this was over, she knew it would be time to settle down, have a family of her own.

But what if this was never over? she asked herself. What if she couldn't find Radick or Waters? What if she couldn't find the resolution, the peace that she needed?

Doubt overwhelmed her. Maybe Dillon was right. Maybe she should let the past go. Just think about the future.

The singing grew louder, seemed to resonant inside her, and she absolutely knew she couldn't turn back. In her heart, in her soul, she believed she was doing the right thing. It would be more difficult without Dillon's help, but somehow, she would find Radick, then Waters.

Renewed, she walked to the convenience mart inside the Citco, bought bottled water, a can of soda and a handful of chocolate bars for the drive, then headed back to her motel. Outside her room, she shifted her bag while she dug into her front jeans' pocket for her key, then turned it in the lock.

She'd stepped into the room, barely had time to close the door behind her when the man lunged forward and grabbed her.

Chapter 7

She didn't have time to react. He was just suddenly *there,* with his arms wrapped around her and one latex-gloved hand tightly covering her mouth. She screamed, but the sound was no more than a muffled cry. The bag in her hand dropped to the floor and the can of soda and the bottled water rolled across the carpet.

"Be a good girl and let's make this easy," a deep, gravelly voice said.

Like hell I will.

Rebecca raised her knee, then stomped hard on the man's foot with the heel of her shoes. He swore through his teeth, then lifted her off her feet. Terror snaked through her when he moved toward the bed. She struggled, kicking her legs and trying to free her arms, but he was bigger than her and at least three or four inches taller. His arms were like steel ropes circling her. When he fell forward on the bed with her underneath him, her terror bolted into absolute panic.

Snapping her head down, she managed to free her mouth long enough to latch onto his hand. He hissed in pain, then squeezed her rib cage so hard she couldn't breathe. The room spun, but still she hung on to his hand, sinking her teeth in deeper through the latex glove.

He didn't let go. His arms tightened even more, crushing her until she thought her ribs might crack. Out of air, Rebecca felt herself go limp. She couldn't move, couldn't fight back, couldn't even draw in a breath to scream. He released her when she went still, then rose up over her.

He brought his fist down.

Pain exploded from her jaw to the top of her skull. She heard the sound of her own groan, smelled the heavy scent of tobacco on his breath, then felt his unshaven cheek scraping against her left ear. Bile rose in her throat. He dropped a knee on her back and pinned her to the bed.

"Stupid bitch," he muttered while he examined the hand she'd bitten. "Now you went and made it personal. I'm gonna have to make you pay for that."

Pain blurred her vision, but she could hear him, the wheeze of his rapid breathing, his mumbled swearing as he studied his hand. It took every ounce of strength Rebecca could summon to slide her arm underneath her, to feel her way into the purse sandwiched between her hips and the bed.

Where is it? she thought, choking back a sob. When her hand brushed against the small plastic cylinder in her purse, hope surged through her. She wrapped her fingers tightly around the canister and unlocked the safety button, knew she had to wait until he was closer.

"This is gonna to be more fun that I'd thought," the man snarled, then dropped his body back down on hers. His cheek was against hers again, and he slid his hand around to the front of her jeans.

Now!

Jerking her arm upward, she twisted her hand at the same time she turned her head away and closed her eyes. She hit the nozzle on top of the pepper spray.

He howled.

Hands covering his face, he rolled away. Rebecca scrambled up to her knees, then slid off the bed onto the floor. When her fingers brushed against a metal soda can, she closed her hand around it, then rose to her knees and swung it into the man's temple. He groaned loudly at the crunching impact.

"Hey!" Someone from the next room pounded on the wall. "What's going on over there?"

Rebecca mumbled a weak call for help, but she couldn't make her legs move. Hissing in pain, his hands still on his face, the man struggled to his feet. *God, no!* She searched for another weapon, anything, but when the pounding started on the wall again and more yelling, the man stumbled to the door and yanked it open, then ran out.

Rebecca sank down on the floor, sucking desperately needed air into her lungs, then coughing at the residue of pepper spray. A distant voice in her brain told her to call the front desk, but her arm was so heavy that the phone, though only three feet away, might as well have been a mile.

Helpless, the best she could manage to do was close her eyes and pray he wouldn't come back.

The small blue sedan Dillon had borrowed from Ilene screeched around the corner and flew into the parking lot of the Mesa Motel. He spotted Rebecca's white rental, and his first reaction was relief he'd caught her before she left. But when he saw her motel room door wide open, a bad feeling snaked up his spine. He pulled sideways into a parking spot and slammed on the brakes, then cut the engine at the same time he jumped out of the car. When he spotted a hand-print of blood on the door, his heart leaped into his throat.

Ignoring the pain shooting through his knee, Dillon sprinted into the room. He saw her lying on the floor, crumpled into a ball. She wasn't moving.

Sweet Jesus.

He dropped down beside her, touched two fingers to her neck. Felt the steady pound of her pulse. *Thank God…*

"Rebecca." He lifted her into his arms, his stomach clenching at the red welt on her chin. He managed to keep his voice calm, called to her again, then released the breath he'd been holding when her eyelids fluttered open. Her eyes were unfocused, her face ashen. He quickly scanned her body for any wounds, but saw no signs of any blood.

"Rebecca, can you—"

"Noooo." She lashed out at him unexpectedly, gave him a healthy jab on his jaw with her fist, then made a weak attempt to push him away. *"No, no, no!"*

"Rebecca." He gripped her shoulders tightly. "It's Dillon. You're safe now."

She stilled, and the clarity slowly returned in her eyes. "Dillon?"

He sat on the floor beside her and pulled her onto his lap, then repeated softly, "You're safe now."

Slowly, she relaxed in his arms, then dropped her head on his shoulder. She started to shake violently. "He—was behind the door—I didn't see him—he was going to—"

"Ssh." He stroked her hair. "We'll talk about it later. Just tell me if you're hurt."

"Just my jaw." She gulped in a lungful of air. "He didn't have time to do anything else."

Relief coursed through his veins. He wanted to pull her closer to him, but was afraid he might crush her if he did. He touched a thumb to the side of her cheek and wiped away a spot of blood. She looked at his hand, then closed her eyes and buried her face against his chest.

"I bit him," she whispered.

"Good girl."

"And I got him in the face with pepper spray." She opened her eyes and her words were stronger this time, edged with satisfaction.

Dillon raised a brow, then placed a light kiss on her temple. "Remind me never to tangle with you."

As badly as he wanted to be out looking for the bastard who'd done this, Dillon knew he had to be here, knew he couldn't leave her. He rocked her until her shaking eased, stroked her back, and slowly he felt her strength seep back into her body.

With a deep sigh, she lifted her head and looked at him. Her eyes were clear now, and some of the color was back in her cheeks. "I just left you in the hospital. What are you doing here?"

"My accident this morning." He tucked a loose strand of hair behind her ear. So soft, he thought. So sweet. He fought back the rage threatening to erupt. Later, he thought. He'd deal with his own emotions later. "I realized it wasn't an accident."

"Ah, is there a problem in here?" a man asked from the open doorway.

Dillon glanced up at the long-limbed young man standing just outside the room. The gold-tone badge on his buttoned-up white polo shirt identified him as the motel's assistant manager. He stayed on the sidewalk outside, his eyes bulging as he glanced nervously from Dillon to Rebecca.

"She was attacked. Call Sheriff Keber." Scooping Rebecca up in his arms, Dillon stood. When the kid continued to stare, Dillon snapped, "Now, dammit!"

The young man moved so fast he tripped over his own big feet, then quickly recovered and ran for the front office. Dillon kicked the door shut, then gently set Rebecca on the bed. A hissing sound caught his attention and he realized a dented soda can lay on the floor and the soda was slowly seeping out onto the carpet.

"I hit him with that after the pepper spray," Rebecca said, hugging her arms tightly around her. She looked at Dillon and he could see a flicker of fight in her green eyes. "I wish it had been a brick."

"That's the spirit." He took her hand in his and pressed a quick kiss to her knuckles. "It's going to get crazy around here in a few minutes. You up for it?"

She nodded slowly. "Will you…can you…"

Her voice trailed off, and she looked away. He sat on the bed beside her and slipped an arm around her shoulders. "I'm staying."

With those two words hovering between them, Rebecca relaxed against him and they waited.

Teresa walked into The Women's Wellness Clinic and stood in a line to speak to the receptionist. The small waiting area looked similar to the one Teresa had been to in San Antonio when she was almost three months pregnant. The clinic that Mitch had taken her to in the hopes that she would change her mind and get an abortion. But looking at all the expectant mothers at the clinic that day had only made her more determined than ever to keep her baby.

Mitch had been furious at her when she wouldn't schedule the surgery. Had eventually even denied that the child was his, though he knew she had never been with any other man before him. She'd been a virgin the night they'd made love the first time. He'd told her how much he loved her, that he wanted to marry her, that he adored her. He was so handsome, so charming, and for six months, he'd made her feel as if timid, shy, plain Teresa Bellochio was the only woman in the world. She'd loved him desperately.

But the love she'd felt for Mitch had been shattered the day he'd turned his back on his own child. She'd had to face her parents by herself, had to listen to their angry words, their ultimatum that she give up her child, either by abortion, or adoption. It didn't matter. As long as no one ever knew.

It was the first time she had ever stood up to her parents. Maybe the first time she had stood up to anyone. She'd been frightened—she still was—but her child had given her the strength to pack her bags and leave, the courage to make her own way. The little money she'd had to call her own she took with her, found a small apartment and worked as a waitress to support herself. Knowing she'd have medical expenses and would need some time off after the baby, she'd put in extra hours and had managed to put a little cash away. Until six weeks ago, when she'd fallen asleep sitting at a booth and the night manager fired her.

Teresa had always suspected that her parents

had paid the manager to fire her, thinking that they could force her to give up her child if she had no job or money. But she couldn't prove it, and even if she could, what difference would it make, anyway? She would never go back to her parents' home, just as she would never give up her baby.

"Can I help you?" a woman behind the counter asked. She was older, with skin the color of melted chocolate and friendly brown eyes.

"I'm not sure, but I think I might be having contractions," Teresa said. "I'm from out of town and I don't have a doctor."

"Just fill this out." The receptionist handed Teresa a medical form and a pen. "Bring it back to me and we'll get you in a room."

A few minutes later, Teresa followed a nurse to an examination room and put on the gown she gave her. Another contraction tightened across her lower belly and she breathed with it, slowly, in then out, until the pain passed.

"Please not now," she whispered to her child. "I need to find a job. Find us a place to live."

She looked up at the knock on the door. A balding, thin man with thick glasses came into the room.

"Mrs. Bellochio?"

She met his gaze, refused to be ashamed. "Miss."

Smiling, he stepped into the room. "I'm Dr. Wilson."

* * *

Dillon had certainly been right about things getting crazy. Within seconds, a group of motel guests and staff started to gather on the sidewalk outside. When Sheriff Keber arrived ten minutes later, he "deputized" the assistant manager to keep everyone away from the door. The young man took his duty seriously and every so often Rebecca could hear him tell people to step back and be quiet.

"I never actually saw his face," she told the sheriff, "but he was probably in his late thirties or early forties."

Hands clasped in her lap, she sat on the edge of the bed. Sheriff Keber had pulled a chair up close to her, and every time she paused or drew in a breath to steady herself, he waited patiently, his pen poised over his notebook until she was ready to continue. She'd already recreated the attack for the sheriff, and now she was trying to describe the man.

"I think he was around five foot ten or eleven, with short brown hair," she went on. "He wore a black long-sleeved T-shirt and jeans, and he smelled like strong cigarettes. When he put his cheek against mine, I felt the stubble of a beard."

A shudder ran through her at the memory, and her stomach rolled. She resisted the urge to glance at Dillon, who stood behind her. She knew if she did, she might give in to the tears she'd managed to hold back. He hadn't said a word since the sheriff had come in a few minutes ago, just stood in the corner like a stone statue. Even from across the room, though, she could feel his tension and his anger; it radiated off him like heat off asphalt.

And still, in spite of all that anger under the surface, he'd been remarkably calm on the outside. He'd been so gentle with her when he'd pulled her onto his lap and held her, had so tenderly stroked her hair and whispered to her that she was safe.

She knew it was silly, foolish even, but with Dillon's strong arms around her, she *had* felt safe. Incredibly, wonderfully, safe.

"I really can't remember anything else." She stared down at her hands. "It just happened so fast."

A soft knock at the door made her jump, then Dr. Thompson, carrying a leather bag, stepped into the room. His gaze went directly to Rebecca and the concern in his eyes warmed her.

"Looks like you've drawn a bit of a crowd outside." The doctor closed the door behind him. "Gets any bigger, we'll need a lemonade stand."

From her experience with the doctor barely an hour ago, Rebecca knew the man used humor to diffuse a tense situation. "I'll take mine hard," she said.

"I'm sure we could arrange that." The doctor smiled at her, then looked at the sheriff. "Move over, Joseph. Let me have a look at my girl."

The sheriff rose and the doctor sat, lifted Rebecca's chin, then frowned when he saw the swelling there. "He use his fist on you?"

She nodded, watched the tender concern on the doctor's face turn vicious, then shift quickly back to compassionate again. He pulled a compress out of his bag and slapped it on his knee, then carefully held it to Rebecca's chin. "You find this bastard, Joseph, and then let me have a few minutes with him."

"I'll find him." Dillon stepped out of the shadows in the corner. "And trust me, he'll need a doctor after I do."

"More likely, a mortician, I think." The sheriff studied Dillon for a long moment. "First your accident, now Rebecca. I might be slow, but I'm not stupid. You want to tell me what's going on?"

"Dillon's accident had nothing to do with me being attacked." Rebecca looked into the little flashlight the doctor shone in her eyes. "The two are completely unrelated."

"No, they're not." Dillon moved closer and met the sheriff's steady gaze. "Someone followed Rebecca here."

Rebecca turned her head too quickly, winced at the jolt of pain in her jaw. "What are you talking about?"

"My accident wasn't an accident," he said quietly, shifting his gaze to Rebecca. "Someone wanted me out of the way first."

"What do you mean, first?"

"Before they came after you."

She blinked, long and slow. "Are you saying that this—" she looked at the bed "—this wasn't random?"

Dillon shook his head. "Waters had you followed."

"That can't be." If her head had been spinning before, it went into warp drive now. "I told you, no one knew I was coming here. And even if they did, I've stopped in over a dozen towns, driven at least five hundred miles since I rented a car in Midland. Surely I would have spotted someone following me."

"Were you looking for anyone?" Dillon asked.

"No, but still—"

"If a man like Waters hired someone to tail you," Dillon said, "then trust me, you'd never know."

"You two want to let me in on what the dickens you're talking about?" Sheriff Keber asked. "And who the devil is Waters?"

"He's—" Rebecca hesitated, realized if she explained who Leon Waters was and what he'd done, why she'd really come here, she'd also be revealing Dillon's background, something he'd obviously never wanted made public. She couldn't do that to him. Hadn't she already caused him enough problems simply by coming here? Whatever was said now, whatever happened, would be his call completely. She looked at him, met his dark gaze, silently told him she would say nothing about his past.

He stared at her for a long moment, then, his decision made, turned to the sheriff. "You might want to sit down," he said with a sigh. "It's a long story."

Bible in his hand, he sat in the front pew of The Angel's Shepherd Church, a spot especially reserved for him after he'd paid for the new glass and marble sanctuary last year. Over the past four years, he had donated over a hundred thousand dollars to the ministry, even volunteered at several of the fund-raisers. He'd always kept a low profile, told the church he preferred to remain anonymous, which only elevated his status all the more.

Leland Worthington was a goddamned pillar of the community.

Though he kept his gaze solemnly attentive to the exuberant, booming minister, his mind was on his yacht. His beautiful, beautiful yacht. She'd be ready to sail in five days. He'd already set his course, and his hands itched to take the helm. Just the thought of steering her onto the open sea made him feel giddy.

By now, he was certain his little problem in

West Texas had been resolved. He would close up his law office on Thursday night, and by the time his staff arrived for work on Friday morning, all they would find would be empty desks and file cabinets and paychecks with large bonuses. The extra money would soften the blow of suddenly being unemployed, he'd figured, and would give them less reason to even attempt to find him.

And after all, it *was* the right thing to do wasn't it?

But it was the phone call he'd received about an hour ago that had put him in such a magnanimous mood. One of his contacts had found a perfect match—an eighteen-year-old, eight months pregnant. She was of Italian descent, just arrived in town, poor, but in excellent health, no husband or family, no insurance. And the most amazing part of all—she didn't even know she was having twins.

One boy. One girl.

Leland thought he had to be the luckiest son of a bitch alive.

No. Not luck, he decided, half-listening to the minister expound on the mysterious ways of God's power. Destiny. He glanced down at the bible in his hand. This woman had been sent to him by divine fate. What else could it possibly be?

He would make sure she received the very best care during her delivery. After, she'd be comforted and looked after, reassured that everything would be fine and time would heal all wounds. And because he wasn't completely heartless, she would be well compensated by an unnamed benefactor.

She was young. She'd have more children. She'd forget.

And she'd never know the truth.

Chapter 8

Despite Sheriff Keber's protests that they'd be better off staying in town, Dillon took Rebecca home with him. There was no way he was letting her out of his sight again.

She sat at his kitchen table, one hand lightly stroking Bowie's head. The dog, who would normally bark and jump around like a crazed kangaroo when Dillon came home, had been quiet and calm since they'd walked in a few minutes ago. He hadn't left Rebecca's side.

That makes two of us, pal, Dillon thought.

She'd tried to pretend that she was all right, even wore her best I'm-fine-don't-worry-about-me face, but that face was pale, with circles of exhaustion under her eyes. Dillon pulled his gaze away from the darkening bruise on her chin. He wasn't ready to think about that just yet. Right now, he knew he needed to stay focused on the present.

He opened a cabinet over the sink and pulled out two shot glasses and a Mason jar filled with amber liquid, then sat at the table beside her. He filled both glasses halfway and handed one to her.

"Here."

Rebecca looked from the Mason jar to the shot glass and frowned. "What is it?"

"Drink it." He put the glass in her hand. "You'll feel better."

Bowie raised his head and sniffed, then made a beeline across the room. Rebecca watched the dog's retreat, then looked back at Dillon, her eyes narrowed suspiciously. She brought the glass to her nose.

"Good Lord!" She scrunched up her face. "It smells like yard clippings."

"Drink."

She sipped, then started to choke and shoved the glass back at him. "It *tastes* like yard clippings. I can't possibly drink this."

"Yes, you can." To prove it, he downed the glass

in his own hand, then shoved hers back at her. "It goes down easier in one slug."

"Nothing could possibly make that go down easy." But she hadn't the strength to argue, either. She drew in a deep breath, held it, and emptied the glass.

Her eyes widened, then she covered her mouth and started to cough. "What *is* that?" she asked between gasps for breath.

"Half whiskey." He was already feeling the affects. "Half tea of herbs, bark, and roots."

"Like I said." She shuddered. "Yard clippings."

He smiled, watched the color seep into her cheeks and the light return to her eyes. He twisted around in his chair and pulled a dishcloth out of a drawer, then doused it with the liquid.

"Don't tell me it's a household cleaner, too," she said, watching him suspiciously.

"It's possible. Never tried it." He held the damp cloth to her chin. "Be still."

For once, she did as he said, and he watched the tension slowly ease from her shoulders. "Old family recipe?" she murmured after a moment.

"My grandfather's."

On a sigh, her eyes drifted closed and she leaned into his hand, letting her chin rest in his palm. "Tell me about him."

"His name was Red Feather." The elixir pumped through his blood now, blurring his vision. It would pass, he knew, and when it did, he would see clearly. "I was only eight when he died, but he used to take me into the canyons. He was a shaman."

"A shaman?"

"A spiritual medicine man," he said, simplifying the answer. "He taught me the ways of the old people. Nature is the life giver. Elements, rocks, plants, animals. All have a source of power and energy and are to be respected."

"That's beautiful," Rebecca whispered.

She was beautiful, he thought. Her cheeks were pale pink now, her lips soft and rosy and slightly parted. Lightly, he stroked her cheek with his thumb. Her skin was baby smooth.

"Rebecca."

"Hmm?" Her eyes fluttered open.

"You know that if Waters hired someone to follow you, that means he's worried."

"Why do you think it's Waters, not Radick?"

"Waters and my father were the brains. Radick was a crooked sheriff looking for a way out of his gambling debt. More than likely, he's still gambling and still in debt. Waters on the other hand, is probably still practicing law somewhere under a different name. He would have the most to lose if the authorities catch up with him."

"The man who attacked me." Her gaze dropped

to the glass in her hands. "After I bit him, he said something about me making this personal."

Meaning it was business up until that point, Dillon thought. "You can't go home now, Rebecca. It's too dangerous."

"They won't stop now, will they?" she asked quietly. He shook his head. "I'll put you somewhere safe, until this is over."

She covered his hand with her own. "I can't do that."

He wanted to argue, but he saw the truth in her eyes, knew it in his gut, in his blood, in his soul. They were in this together, had always been. Long before this moment, long before she'd shown up at the Backwater Saloon. Even long before that night twenty-four years ago.

He'd known this was coming. Like a shift in the air before a storm. He'd felt it. Smelled it.

Dreamed it.

Why now? he wondered briefly, but he understood that the answer, whatever it was, would reveal itself in its own time.

The warmth of her smooth hand on his stirred his blood. Her skin was pale against his dark, her fingers long and smooth and soft. Her gaze skimmed his face, worried over the stitches on his forehead, then glanced at his blood-splattered T-shirt. "What now?"

He traced the seam of her lips with his thumb, ached to press his mouth there, ached to take her to his bed and lose himself in her. To offer her comfort and himself release. There would be pleasure for both of them.

A time for every purpose...

With a sigh, he pulled his hand away. "Now you rest for a while. You'll feel better, and then we'll talk."

When she'd closed her eyes, she'd never intended to fall asleep. Wouldn't have thought she could, she'd been so wound up. But the concoction Dillon had given her—as awful as it had been—had apparently done its job. A warm, tingling sensation had crept through her body, the pain in her jaw had eased, then muscle by muscle, she'd slowly relaxed. Lying on his big bed, with his scent enveloping her, she'd drifted off.

And she dreamed. A montage of time-lapse images and sounds. Black, swiftly moving clouds. A white deer in the woods, caught in a hunter's trap. Frothy waves that crashed blue onto a shore, then rolled back the color of blood. A room at the end of a dark corridor. Hands reaching out to her, a woman's hands. Rebecca felt her fear, her pain— pain that gripped across her belly like a vise, squeezing, tightening, then blissfully, thankfully, releasing.

A voice inside her head—two voices—so tiny, so urgent…*please hurry…we need you…*

Gasping, she opened her eyes, felt her heart pumping wildly, as if she'd been running. She'd heard the voices as clearly as if they'd been standing beside her, but no one was there.

A dream. Only a dream.

She glanced at the bedside clock, and though it felt as if she'd been sleeping for hours, only thirty minutes had passed. In spite of the dreams, she felt remarkably rested, her head amazingly clear and the pain in her jaw nearly gone.

She had no idea what was in the concoction Dillon had given her—she probably didn't want to know—but it had certainly worked.

The room was so quiet, so still. She felt a moment of panic, then relaxed when she saw Dillon sitting at the kitchen table, reading. Steam rose off the coffee mug in his left hand. He still wore the same T-shirt and torn jeans from this morning. She looked down at her own disheveled appearance, sighed, then slowly rose.

He lifted his head when she moved beside him.

"Feeling better?" he asked.

Nodding, she glanced down. Her pulse jumped when she realized he wasn't reading a book.

Her mother's journal.

She sank down on the chair beside him. "It was

snowing the day I found it. A soft, pretty snow that covered the trees and front lawn white. My mother had only been gone a few weeks, I wasn't ready to clean out her closet, yet, but I was looking for her favorite sweater, a pale green cashmere. She always knew I coveted that sweater, had told me one day she'd give it to me. I just wanted something of hers, something special."

She'd relived that day at least a hundred times. A thousand. Walking up the sidewalk to the house, her breath rising like smoke in the crisp air. Climbing the stairs, opening the closet door. Flipping on the light. "It was under the sweater, just sitting there."

She would never forget the first line, *It is a horrible, horrible thing I've done.* There'd been exact details, dates, times, names. Places. Three days later, after the last entry, *May God forgive me.*

Dillon closed the journal, then picked up his mug and put it in Rebecca's hand. When she lifted a suspicious brow, he shook his head and grinned. "Just coffee this time."

She sipped, watched the steam rise from the mug. "I understand she must have written it to protect herself and me. But after twenty-four years, why would she keep it? Why would she want me to find it?"

"To do what she couldn't," Dillon said.

Rebecca closed her eyes and whispered, "There are times when I wished I'd never found it. When I wished I'd burned it. No one would have ever known."

"You would."

"Yes." She opened her eyes. "I would."

Bowie, who'd been sleeping on the cool kitchen tile, suddenly lifted his head, then jumped up and ran to the front door. When the loud knock sounded, the dog barked and wagged his tail. Rebecca glanced nervously at Dillon.

"Maria's back from church," he said with a sigh, then stood. "Prepare yourself."

Rebecca had no idea who Maria was or what he meant by "prepare yourself."

Until he opened the door.

A young boy on her heels, the woman blasted into the room, her dress an explosion of blue and yellow flowers. When she saw the stitches on Dillon's forehead, she slapped her hands to her round face, then made a sign of the cross over her ample bosom.

"Dillon! *Dios mío!*"

She spoke in rapid-fire Spanish, but other than "Dr. Thompson," something about a woman named Lidia, and *"teléfono,"* Rebecca had no idea what the woman was saying.

"I'm fine, Maria," Dillon said, then looked at

the child, who stared wide-eyed at the blood on Dillon's T-shirt and jeans. "*Estoy bien,* Juan."

The gentle tone in Dillon's voice when he spoke to the boy surprised Rebecca. It seemed that the man who wanted no ties or relationship to anyone, had one after all.

"You are fine?" Maria threw up her hands in exasperation. "You do not look fine to me. You look like the piñata at Juan's birthday party last week. And your head must be just as empty. Why are you here and not at the hospital?"

Before Dillon could answer, Maria launched into another lecture in a mix of English and Spanish. "Stubborn man," "fool," and "sense of a fence post," were just a few of the words Rebecca managed to understand.

Maria's gaze shifted to the kitchen table and her jaw went slack when she saw Dillon had company. Rebecca drew in a breath and held it.

Quickly, quietly, Dillon spoke to the woman in Spanish, obviously explaining what had happened at the motel. Her brow tightly furrowed, Maria listened intently, then crossed herself again before she hurried across the room.

"*Pobrecita!*" Maria took Rebecca's hand in her own. "I would kill the bastard myself."

While Maria fussed over her, Dillon closed the door and said something to the boy Rebecca couldn't hear, but it made the child smile. When Dillon put his hand out, Juan slapped it with his own.

"Come sit on the sofa," Maria insisted, gently pulling Rebecca up from the chair. "Juan, bring pillows from the bed. Dillon, it is too hot and too bright in here, turn on the air conditioner and dim the lights."

Rebecca glanced at Dillon, who simply shrugged, then, like Juan, did as he was told. With a silent sigh, Rebecca resigned herself to Maria's well-intentioned clucking and let the woman lead her to the sofa. For the next few minutes, Maria fluffed pillows and adjusted cushions and genuinely fretted over Rebecca.

"I will make *arroz con pollo* for you." For at least the tenth time, Maria plumped the pillow she'd slipped behind Rebecca's back. "And *chile rellenos*. My late husband, Pablo, said my *chile rellenos* could make a grown man cry."

Rebecca could easily imagine Maria making a grown man cry. Even Dillon had moved to the kitchen and stayed as far out of the woman's way as the room would allow. Holding a cup of coffee, he stood at the counter, amusement in his dark eyes as he watched Maria fidgeting about. Rebecca glared at him over Maria's head, did her best to dissuade Maria from going to any trouble, but the woman quickly dismissed Rebecca's protests.

"It is settled. You will rest while I cook." Maria, content that she finally had Rebecca settled, turned her sights on Dillon and moved into the kitchen. "Dillon, *quítate la ropa*."

Dillon spit out the coffee he'd just sipped. "What?"

"You heard me." Maria folded her arms. "Take off your clothes. I will wash and sew them for you."

"I will not." His eyes narrowed dangerously.

A lesser woman might have backed off, but not Maria.

She reached for the snap on Dillon's jeans.

"Maria!" Dillon fumbled the coffee cup into the sink and pushed the woman's hands away. "For God's sake!"

She faced him down. "I've seen a naked man before, *chistoso*."

"Not this man," Dillon argued.

Shaking her head, Maria looked at Rebecca. "Was he this shy when you two were *amantes*?"

Uh oh. Rebecca wasn't completely certain what the word meant, but the expression on Dillon's face gave her a pretty good idea.

Lovers.

"Who told you that?" Dillon asked sharply.

"Everyone in town knows you broke this woman's heart when you left her. Such a sweet, beautiful girl." Maria shook her head in disgust. "You should be ashamed."

"That does it." Dillon walked to a chest of drawers, pulled out a clean pair of jeans and a T-shirt, then went into the bathroom and slammed the door behind him.

Maria turned back to Rebecca and sighed. "Such fire. Such *pasión*. My Fernando and I shared that once."

"I thought your husband's name was Pablo," Rebecca said.

"It was," Maria replied with a twinkle in her eyes. "But Fernando was my first love. Such men are few, are they not?"

Rebecca had no answer for that, and even if she had, she certainly wouldn't have responded with Juan in the room. The boy stood by the sofa, staring at her. When Rebecca looked at him, he blushed, then quickly glanced down.

A crash sounded from the bathroom, then a string of expletives. Bowie ran to the closed door and barked at it. A moment later, the door opened, the jeans and T-shirt flew out, then the door slammed shut again.

"*Muy caliente.*" Maria smiled and kissed her fingertips. "*Muy hombre.* Come, Juan, we will roast peppers for the *rellenos*. Bowie—" Maria clapped for the dog "—I have a big soup bone for you. Come."

Dog and child followed the woman out of the room. Rebecca listened to the quiet in their wake and decided this had to be what it felt like after a tornado had passed.

To say the least, Maria Guadalupe was an interesting woman.

The bathroom door opened a moment later, and Dillon stuck his head out. "Please tell me she's gone."

Rebecca bit her lip to keep from laughing. For all his tough guy, lone wolf bullpuckey, Dillon Blackhawk, *muy hombre,* was afraid of a middle-aged grandmother.

He emerged from the bathroom wearing a white T-shirt and faded, but clean jeans. With a sigh, he sat next to her on the sofa, then reached up and twisted a strand of her hair around his finger.

She held her breath.

"So we were lovers, were we?" he murmured.

"I didn't *exactly* tell anyone that." How could such a simple touch make her skin vibrate? Make her want to lean in closer. "I just sort of mentioned to Dixie and Jennie that we knew each other."

"And let them come to their own conclusion."

"I can talk to them," Rebecca offered. "Explain that I gave them the wrong idea."

"I don't give a damn what anyone thinks, Rebecca, and certainly not Dixie or Jennie."

"What about Ilene?" The question was out before she could stop it. *Damn!*

His hand stilled. "What about Ilene?"

"Nothing," she said quickly.

"More conclusions." He shook his head. "Ilene and I were never lovers."

When he slid his fingertip over the top of her ear and tucked her hair back, Rebecca felt her pulse skip. "Oh."

"And that's where the difference is between you and Ilene." His voice softened, and he lowered his gaze to her mouth. "You and I *are* going to be lovers."

Her pulse went into a full, breath-stealing sprint at his statement. She might have argued, could have—*should* have—been indignant. But she didn't. And she wasn't.

Because she knew it was true.

"You need to rest now." He lifted his gaze back to hers. "We'll have Maria to deal with tonight, then a long day ahead of us tomorrow."

"Tomorrow?" It took her a long moment to make the transition back to reality, then another moment just to remember to breathe. "What are we doing tomorrow?"

Though a smile lifted one corner of his mouth, his eyes glinted like black ice. "We're gonna find us a bookie."

* * *

He wished to God he hadn't accepted Reverend Graybelle's invitation to Sunday dinner at the country club. He could think of a dozen places, a hundred places, he'd rather be than sitting next to Katherine Graybelle while she babbled on about an upcoming fundraiser in the fall.

She wasn't a bad-looking woman, Leland thought. Blond hair, big, blue eyes, a great pair of tits, but so freaking uptight the reverend probably needed the Jaws of Life to get her legs apart. And besides that, he figured she had to be pushing forty. The way he saw it, by the time most women reached thirty-five, they were pretty much used up.

"The committee had so many good ideas," Katherine flittered on. "But we finally decided to have a silent auction."

Well, that let's you out, Leland thought, carefully holding his smile in place while he sipped on a glass of champagne. The woman hadn't shut up for a moment since they'd all sat at the reverend's table in the elegant dining room.

"We know how busy you are, Leland." Smiling, Katherine leaned in. "But we were hoping you might find it in your schedule, and your Christian heart, to donate an hour or two of legal estate planning."

He looked at the hand Katherine had placed on his arm. He'd be damned if she wasn't flirting with him, right in front of her own husband—a god-damned minister, no less—who was currently in an intense political discussion with one of the church elders. Leland took a closer look at the woman. Even if she was a little old and talked too much, maybe under that uptight, lily-white facade, she was a hot number, just waiting for the right man to ring her own private little church bell.

"I'd be delighted to help." He smiled at the blonde. Hell, he'd be long gone by the end of the week, anyway. He could promise her the frigging moon. And if he got a little something in return to send him on his way, so much the better. "Why don't you stop by my office tomorrow afternoon, say around four, and I can write something up for you."

He'd send his secretary and paralegal both home at four and have the office all to himself.

"You're such a generous man," Katherine said, blushing. "How can we ever thank you for all you've done?"

He envisioned the woman thanking him tomorrow, on her knees, but the vibration of his cell phone in his sport coat interrupted his thoughts.

"Excuse me." He glanced at the display on his phone. *Edmunds.* About damn time. He looked back up at Katherine and did his best to look contrite. "I've been waiting for a call from my sister about our mother. She's been ill."

"I'm so sorry." Worry creased Katherine's brow. "I'll say a prayer for her."

"Thank you." His mother had been dead for ten years, but if Katherine thought he needed comforting, it would be that much easier, and quicker, to get the reverend's wife naked and on her back. "That means so much to me."

When he was in the hallway outside the dining room, he answered the phone and clenched his jaw while Edmunds talked.

"I see," Leland said calmly several times, though inside he burned with rage. *Idiot!* he wanted to scream. *Moron!* But there were people walking by, people he knew, and all he could do was smile and nod. "Yes, well, I have complete trust that you can handle the situation. Tell Mom I love her."

Though he wanted to kick something, Leland prided himself on his composure when he snapped his phone shut and strolled back to the dining room. He'd make his excuses, tell the reverend and Mrs. Graybelle how sorry he was, and leave.

He'd lost his appetite, for food and for the reverend's wife.

Chapter 9

With a dull ache in his head and a stiff shoulder from sleeping on the sofa, Dillon woke just before dawn. He sat, rolled his neck until it gave a nice crack, then stretched his shoulders and stood, putting weight on the knee he'd hit yesterday. He might have to be careful with it for a couple of days, but considering the condition of his truck, he supposed he was lucky. Not that someone trying to run him off the road was exactly lucky.

He wanted blood, could practically taste it. Not for himself or his truck, but for Rebecca. Dillon's eyes narrowed. When he found the guy who'd broken into her room and attacked her—and he *would* find him—there was no question in his mind that blood would be spilled.

He looked forward to it.

He'd made a couple of phone calls last night while Rebecca had been preoccupied with Maria. He figured he'd at least be prepared for whatever— or whomever—might turn up around the next cor- ner. It was the first time since his father had died that he'd had need of the vast resources available to him, and he hadn't hesitated to use them.

Whatever it took, he would see this through.

Bowie, who'd been sleeping at the foot of the bed, rose and stretched, then padded to the door to be let outside. This had been their routine for the past four months, one they had both been comfort- able enough with.

A routine that was about to change, Dillon noted and glanced at Rebecca.

It was the second time in the past twenty-four hours that he'd watched her sleep. But it was dif- ferent this time. This time she was in *his* bed.

They'd locked horns over it last night when he'd told her she was sleeping in the bed, but he'd won, of course. After the day she'd had, she'd simply been too tired to argue with any real heat.

She lay on her stomach, hugging the pillow under her head, her hair falling like a curtain over half her face. One long, tempting leg had slipped out from under the blanket covering her and hung over the edge of the mattress.

One *bare* leg, he noted, taking in the slender curve of calf and well-toned thigh.

His blood stirred.

He knew she wore white running shorts and an oversized pink T-shirt under that blanket, not the sexy little number she'd had on in her motel room. He'd watched her rummage through her suitcase last night, seen the hesitation in her eyes as she'd looked down at the slacks and blouse she wore, then glance nervously over her shoulder at him. It didn't take a mind reader to know she was debating whether she should sleep in her clothes or not. After a long, internal discussion with herself, she'd opted for the shorts and T-shirt.

Yesterday, when he'd told her that they would be lovers, her breath had caught and her eyes had widened. But she hadn't disputed it. She knew it, too.

It was simply a matter of when.

He watched her shift from her stomach to her side, then softly sigh as she curled a hand to her slender neck. In sleep, she looked like a fairy-tale princess waiting for a kiss from a prince to wake her. A mass of chestnut curls fanned her heart-shaped face. Thick, dark lashes lay against her smooth, milk-white skin. Her lips were her only feature that didn't fit into the fairy-tale picture.

They were too sexy, too seductive. It was damn hard to look at that mouth and not want to dive into the heady taste of her again.

He moved beside the bed and whispered her name. She didn't respond, just sighed again and rolled to her back, sliding one of her arms over her head. A jolt of lust shot through him.

"Rebecca," he repeated, louder.

Frowning, she rolled back to her side and mumbled something. When the blanket slipped off, revealing more bare skin and the curve of her breasts, Dillon clenched his jaw. Apparently, Sleeping Beauty needed a kiss to wake up, he thought.

Too bad he wasn't a prince.

Turning away, he walked to the door and opened it. Bowie bounded in and ran straight for the bed. At the first sloppy lick on her cheek, Rebecca shrieked, then sat, clutching the blanket to her. Thinking that Rebecca wanted to play, Bowie tugged harder on the blanket, growling and shaking his head.

"Bowie!" Rebecca struggled with the dog. "Stop!"

Smiling, Dillon leaned against his kitchen counter, watching the battle between the beast and the beauty.

Beauty lost when the beast finally yanked the

blanket away, then ran across the room and dropped it. Wagging his tail, ears pricked upward, Bowie dropped down on his front legs and barked again, hoping Rebecca would come after him.

Apparently, she didn't feel like playing.

Raking her hands through her hair, Rebecca sat on the edge of the bed and glared at Dillon. "Is that how you always wake up your overnight guests?"

"We've never had an overnight guest before." He looked at Bowie, who was still waiting for Rebecca to come chase him. "Have we, pal?"

"Well, it's no wonder." Rebecca wiped at the cheek Bowie had licked. "You could certainly both use an etiquette lesson."

"Wish I'd caught it on video." Chuckling he turned and pulled a can of coffee out of the cupboard. "You should have seen your face."

"You're a sick man, Dillon Blackhawk. A sick, twisted man who—"

When she didn't finish, Dillon turned. Rebecca had frozen on the edge of the bed, her eyes staring blankly.

"Rebecca?"

She didn't answer him, just continued to stare at nothing. Her eyes were wide, unseeing, her breathing shallow. Then suddenly, on a gasp, she wrapped her arms around her middle and leaned forward.

He dropped the can of coffee onto the counter

and hurried to the bed, sat beside her and took hold of her arms. Her skin felt cool and clammy. "What's wrong?"

She shuddered, then blinked several times and her gaze met his. "Dillon?"

"Are you all right?"

"I—I—yes, I'm fine." She drew in a deep breath, then lifted a shaky hand to her forehead. "That was weird."

Her eyes were lucid now, he noted, her skin warming. "What happened?"

"I have no idea. I can't really explain it. I was here, and then suddenly I wasn't." Closing her eyes, she slowly shook her head. "All I remember was a bright light and pain. It's gone now."

He rubbed her arms, felt her relax under his touch. "Where was the pain?"

"Low and across my stomach. Very intense. It was the oddest thing, but it was like it was—" She looked away and shook her head. "Never mind. It's silly."

"What?" He put a finger under her chin and lifted her face. "What was it like?"

She met his gaze and frowned. "Like I was someone else."

It was the worst one yet.

Teresa breathed with the contraction, slowly,

deeply, again and again, focused her attention completely on the overhead light. When it finally passed, she closed her eyes and sagged limply back on the bed.

In spite of the fact her due date was still four weeks away, it seemed that her baby had different plans.

She glanced around the private room she'd been transferred to sometime during the past few hours. It was a nice room, with a warm, homey feeling, instead of the sterile environment of a hospital or clinic. The walls were soft green, the lights dim, soft music played from an overhead speaker. It even had a private bath.

It was odd that she'd slept through the transfer, but she had been unusually tired since the doctor had ordered an IV after his examination yesterday. She'd also been hooked to a monitoring device. The doctor had assured her that even though she was going into labor early, her baby had a strong, healthy heartbeat and everything looked great.

Teresa had continued to dose off and on, and because there were no windows and no clock in the room, she'd lost her sense of time. For the past few hours, a nurse named Elena had come in every few minutes to check on her. She was a small woman, Hispanic, with warm hands and a soft, soothing voice. She'd sat and talked with her for a while, asked if there was any family or friends, anyone at all, that she could call. Though it had been embarrassing, Teresa had admitted she was completely alone, that she had no money. Elena had simply smiled and told her not to worry, that the clinic was run by donations, and that women in her position were eligible not only for free medical expenses, but assistance after the baby was born, as well. Elena had even told her that they could help her find a place to live.

Teresa had cried tears of joy. Knew that her prayers had been answered.

She felt another contraction sneaking up on her and breathed with it, focusing once again on the soft light overhead. The contractions had no rhythm yet, though they seemed to be coming with more frequency and had also grown slightly in intensity. The last time the doctor had checked her, maybe an hour ago, she had only been dilated to three. He had told her she would have a ways to go yet, then had given her something in the IV that would speed up the labor.

The contraction slowly passed, and she closed her eyes on a heavy sigh. Lovingly, Teresa ran her hand over her swollen belly. She was frightened, knew the next few hours would be difficult, but the thought of holding her baby, of kissing its tiny cheek, kept her strong.

"It won't be long, sweetheart," she whispered. "Mommy loves you."

Shifting her weight in the bed, Teresa started to sit, then gasped at the rush of warm liquid between her legs. Her heart pounding furiously, Teresa pulled the sheets away, but with her stomach and the wires attached to the monitor, it was hard to see anything. She pushed the button for the nurse, and Elena hurried into the room.

"Something happened," Teresa said frantically. "Something's wrong."

Elena looked down, then smiled and shook her head. "Nothing's wrong, honey. Your water just broke."

They were showered, packed and ready to go by eight o'clock. Not that Dillon had exactly "packed," Rebecca thought while she zipped up her own suitcase. He'd shoved a few articles of clothing in a sports bag, grabbed a large round plastic container of dog food and a bowl, then told her to meet him out front when she was ready.

For now, she knew she needed to let him call the shots. There was no question she was in way over her head, and she was certainly out of her element. Coming into this mess, she'd been stupid and naive. She'd had one hell of a crash course yesterday. She'd learned fast and hard, but she'd learned.

Touching her chin, she thought about the man who'd attacked her, remembered the press of his knee in her back and the smell of cigarettes on his breath.

She knew she should be afraid. But she wasn't. She was angry. And more determined than ever.

At the sound of a horn honking, she picked up her suitcase, then heard the sound of Juan laughing in the front yard when she stepped outside. It had taken Rebecca nearly an hour of interaction with the boy last night before he'd even look her in the eye, then another hour of playing a hand-held video game before he'd began to laugh and speak to her. She realized she'd miss him, and Maria, who'd spent the entire evening feeding and mothering both her and Dillon—much to his discomfort.

Spending time with Maria had made Rebecca painfully aware of how much she'd missed her own mother. There'd been so little time to grieve before she'd found the journal, and now here she was, with Dillon, in Texas, about as far from her safe little world as she could possibly get.

When she stepped through the gate, Bowie galloped to her, barked a greeting, then galloped back to the street where a brand new, glossy-black crew cab pickup with shiny chrome wheels was parked at the curb. Based on the lack of license plates, it was right off the showroom floor. Juan was sitting in the driver's seat, bouncing up and down, his small hands on the wheel. Dillon stood at the open passenger door beside Maria.

How had he done that? she wondered, staring in disbelief at the black behemoth. It would be one thing if they were in the city, but Resolute was at least a hundred miles away from any dealership. And on top of that, it was only eight in the morning.

Still, a man with forty million dollars at his disposal could move mountains if he wanted to, she supposed. And if there was anything at all she'd learned about Dillon, it was to expect the unexpected.

"Look at me, Rebecca." Juan laughed and cranked the wheel back and forth. "I'm driving!"

"You look very handsome driving, Juan." Rebecca looked at the boy and smiled. When he beamed at her, she felt her heart melt.

"Can you believe an insurance company would send a replacement so quickly?" Maria said, her eyes wide. "I have never seen anything like it."

"Me, either." Rebecca looked at Dillon. In the morning light, she could see that the swelling had gone down on his eye, but the bruising had settled into a bluish purple that looked as if he'd stepped into a meat packer's fist. "That must be quite a policy to provide this kind of service."

"It cost a little extra," Dillon said with a shrug.

Yeah, like around forty thousand dollars extra, she thought.

"You ready?" he asked her.

She glanced up and down the street. "Where's my rental?"

"Handled."

She raised a brow, but there was no point in questioning him. Apparently, he was a man who knew how to get things done.

Rebecca moved into Maria's open arms and hugged her. "Thank you so much for everything."

"De nada." Maria smiled. "There is always a place for you at *mi casa*."

Rebecca hadn't time to reply before Juan jumped out of the cab and threw his arms around Dillon's waist. Stunned at the unexpected display of emotion from the child, Dillon tensed, then slowly bent and hugged the boy back.

"I'll be back in a few days," he said, ruffling Juan's hair. *"Te doy mi palabra.* Will you watch my things for me?"

Pleased to be given such an important job, Juan pulled away and straightened his shoulders, then quickly nodded. Dillon stood and whistled for Bowie, who came running from across the street. The dog jumped into the back seat of the pickup and barked, then looked anxiously at Dillon, as if to say, "What are you waiting for? Let's go!"

After Rebecca climbed in the front seat and buckled in, Maria picked up a small cooler sitting on the curb and handed it to Dillon, then grabbed him in a bear hug. There were tears in her eyes when she finally pulled away and tenderly touched his cheek. *"Vio con dios, miho."*

Embarrassed, Dillon tolerated another hug and a kiss on the cheek from Maria, then moved around the truck, set the cooler on the floor of the back seat and slid behind the wheel. Maria and Juan waved as they drove away, then Juan broke loose and ran down the street, still waving when they turned the corner.

When Dillon pulled onto the highway and punched the engine, it roared like an animal being released from its cage. The smell of new leather and man was a heady mix, Rebecca thought, and with all the muscle surrounding her, she felt a bit intimidated, yet excited at the same time. She glanced sideways at Dillon. His attention was focused on the road, one large hand resting confidently on the steering wheel while he pushed buttons on the radio, searching for a station. His profile was as handsome as the front of his face. Strong, square jaw, high cheekbones, that dark, intense gaze that could cut a man off at the feet and make women weak in the knees.

You and I are going to be lovers.

His words shivered through her, made her skin tingle and her breasts tighten and ache.

Determined to get her mind off the physical aspect of her relationship with Dillon, she forced her mind back to the reason that had brought her here. "Where are we going?"

"Flat Falls."

"Flat Falls?"

"It's north of here, about three hundred miles. Radick lived there until he was thirty, then he moved to Wolf River and was sheriff for three years." Dillon flipped on the radio, searched for a station. "He left Wolf River shortly after my aunt and uncle's accident and basically dropped off the face of the earth."

She remembered everything he'd learned about her and she couldn't decide if it made her feel safe, or frightened. "How do you know these things?"

He glanced briefly at her before settling on Tom Petty singing "American Girl," then leaned back comfortably. "I made a few connections when I was in the military."

The military. That would certainly explain the missing years after Dillon had left Wolf River. "What kind of connections?"

He changed lanes and zipped past a slow-moving cattle truck. "It means I know people who have access to information."

"Oh." The comment raised dozens of questions, but his tone and facial expression more than suggested she not ask. "So you think Radick went back to his roots, then?"

"We gotta start somewhere," he said with a shrug. "Right now, it's as good a place as any."

She supposed it was. It certainly made sense. As a rule, people had a tendency to return to what they were most familiar with, what made them comfortable.

She hoped when it came to Spencer Radick, the rule would hold true.

It had been a good day.

Leland checked his bank account online and smiled at the money that Antonio had transferred into a special account. It was only half the amount they'd agreed upon, but the balance would be deposited when the babies were delivered.

The Bellochio woman was progressing nicely with her labor. An hour ago, her water had broke, she'd dilated to four and the odds were high that the babies would be born today. Leland had already made arrangements for the exchange and had even ordered a box of Cuban cigars for Antonio and a huge flower arrangement for his wife. Gifts for the proud parents.

Everything was finally falling into place for

him. Even the problem with that annoying Blake woman and Dillon Blackhawk had finally been resolved.

Leland looked at all the zeros on the balance in his Swiss bank account, then leaned back in his desk chair and smiled.

He didn't have a fucking care in the world.

Two hours after they'd left Resolute, Dillon pulled into a public rest stop beside a small man-made lake. In front of the restrooms, a young couple stood beside a motor home studying a map, and at the far edge of the gravel parking lot, two old geezers were bent over the open hood of a white truck hauling a fishing boat.

"Five minutes." Dillon rolled the windows down and cut the engine.

"Gosh, why so long?" Rebecca asked with sweet sarcasm. "And here I thought you were in a hurry."

The look he gave her was bland. Chuckling, she slid out of the front seat and sashayed toward the restrooms. When she tripped on a rock in the dirt, it was his turn to chuckle. She glowered at him over her shoulder, then straightened her back and disappeared inside the square concrete block structure.

He was thankful that she hadn't tried to make small talk for the past two hours. He was used to traveling alone, used to going where he wanted, when he wanted, and not having to think about anyone but himself. If it had been up to him, he would have driven straight through to Flat Falls, stopping only for gas. But between Rebecca's growling stomach and Bowie's growing restlessness, Dillon had been reluctantly forced to pull into the rest stop.

He stepped out of the truck and stretched his stiff leg, then opened the back door. Bowie shot out of the truck like an arrow and headed straight for the lake where a flock of ducks smoothly glided across the water. Clearly unconcerned with the barking beast, the birds turned their backs to the dog and calmly swam to the opposite shore. The ducks' indifference provoked Bowie all the more and he ran around to the other side of the lake, only to have the small flock turn away again.

Pulling the cooler out of the back seat, Dillon headed for the shade of an oak tree. Though it was only midmorning, the heat already shimmered in the heavy, humid air. Storm coming in, Dillon thought, noting the clouds on the surrounding, low-lying mountains. If they were lucky, they'd stay ahead of it.

While he waited for dog and woman to join him, he sat on the ground, then dug a bottle of water and a burrito out of the cooler. When he spotted the plastic baggie filled with Maria's famous chocolate chip cookies, he smiled. The woman could tempt the devil himself with those cookies. He ate one in two bites, then stretched out his legs and dug into a burrito. Bowie, resigned to the fact that he couldn't reach the ducks, had run off to explore a small outcropping of rocks several yards away.

Sitting on the ground, under the shade of a tree, with the scent of a storm brewing in the distance, Dillon thought of the first time his grandfather had taken him into The Canyon. Dillon had only been seven, but he could still hear his grandfather's whisper, *"Listen, Lakota. If you are truly quiet, you can hear the ants talk to each other. Listen."* And Dillon *had* heard the ants. And the rabbit, and the spider. Even the canyon walls themselves had spoken that day.

There'd been many lessons in The Canyon the year before Red Feather had died. The rambling of a crazy old Indian, Dillon had heard some people say in later years.

But crazy or not, he'd loved his grandfather. And for Dillon, that was enough.

The sound of tires on gravel caught his attention. A white SUV with tinted windows had pulled into the rest stop parking lot at the same time Rebecca came out of the restroom. Dillon tensed, then relaxed when a couple of teenage boys piled out of the back seat. Rebecca smiled at the teenagers and said hello. After she'd walked past them, they turned and stared openly at her butt. If they hadn't been so young, Dillon might have been more annoyed, but Rebecca's round bottom in a snug pair of jeans was impossible to ignore.

He watched her walk toward him, sleek curves, full breasts, long legs. A smile lingered on that sexy mouth of hers and fire danced in her hair under the sunlight. She sank down beside him, pulled out a water for herself and took a delicate sip, then recapped the bottle. When he watched her tongue lick her lips, the blood in the top half of his body instantly went south.

Ignoring the tightening in his groin, he handed her a burrito. "We won't stop again, so eat now, and unless you want to look for rocks along the side of the road, don't drink too much water."

"Spoken with such eloquence." Though her tone was sarcastic, there was a smile in her eyes as she unwrapped the foil on her food. "Where's Bowie?"

Dillon leaned back against the trunk of the tree. "Looking for snakes and varmints."

"Same as us." Sobered by her own words, Rebecca stared at the burrito in her hand. "What if we find Radick?" she asked quietly. "What then?"

"We're going to ask him real nice to tell us where Waters is."

"What if he doesn't know?"

"Then we'll keep asking him until he does."

She swallowed hard. "You mean you would—"

When she stopped, he sighed. "Rebecca, someone ran me off the road and attacked you. Someone who might very well pop back up at any moment and try to get it right the second time. That makes me more than a little cranky."

At the sound of ducks quacking, Dillon glanced toward the lake. Bowie had waded into the water a few feet and gotten closer to the ducks than they'd liked. He watched the drama, ready to intercede if necessary, but Bowie finally turned around and came splashing out of the lake again.

"I'll do what I have to do," he said and looked back at her. "If you can't handle that, I need to know right now."

Her gaze held steady with his, and her eyes sparked green. "I can handle it."

"All right, then." He flattened the empty water bottle in his hand and tossed it into a trash can several feet away. "Finish eating and let's do it."

Chapter 10

They left the interstate past Sweetwater and headed north on the highway. The land surrounding them was as sparse as it was desolate, with sharp-edged mesas of eroding rock and spine-covered cactus. In the distance, like the naked spine of a massive dinosaur, dark brown hills rumbled across the horizon.

When the sign emerged from the sun-baked dirt: Flat Falls, Next Right, Dillon turned off the highway.

Gunmetal gray clouds had swelled and nipped at their heels since they'd left the rest stop, but they'd managed to stay ahead of the storm. With luck, they'd be back on the road long before the rain started.

Flat Falls wasn't much bigger than Resolute, which was a plus on their side, but Dillon knew that asking questions in a town where everyone knew everyone else could be a dangerous thing.

"Where do we start?" Rebecca asked, nervously biting her lip.

"Same place you started with me." He pulled into a weed-choked asphalt parking lot beside a dive called The Red Eye and parked.

"A bar?" She glanced at the dashboard clock. "At one o'clock in the afternoon?"

The look he gave her was tolerant. He pulled a small cell phone out of the glove box and tucked it into the front pocket of his jeans. "Give me your phone."

She rooted through her purse, then handed him her phone. He scrolled through the menu, entered his number and handed it back to her. "If there's a problem, call me."

"What do you mean?" She frowned at him. "I'm coming with you."

"This isn't a cocktail party or debutante's ball, sweetheart. You walk in there with me and I guarantee you there'll be an outbreak of lockjaw."

"But you can't expect me to—"

"I can and you will." He put enough heat behind the words to make her shoulders stiffen. "You can leave the engine on and run the air conditioner or take Bowie for a walk and find some shade. Keep your cell phone on, just in case I need to call you."

"You don't even know my number," she said when he opened the truck door and stepped out.

"I know it."

The Red Eye was no different than any other hole-in-the-wall bar Dillon had ever walked into. Dark. Stale air, thick with cigarette smoke. Even the clientele looked the same, he thought, scanning the room. Cowboys nursing their beers. Bikers talking to a couple of working girls. A man and woman sitting next to each other in a corner booth, probably married, but not to each other.

A baseball game was playing on the wall-mounted television over the counter, a replay of an Astros game from the night before, Dillon realized as he slid onto a bar stool. Mouth open, eyes squinting, the bartender stared at the TV.

"Anything on draft?"

"Nope." The open mouth moved, but the eyes stayed on the television.

"Shiner Bok, then."

Eyes still on the game, the bartender reached under the counter, pulled out a bottle and popped the cap, then slid it across the bar.

Tossing back a swallow of beer, Dillon lifted his gaze to the television. "You gonna have the game on here tonight?"

"Damn straight," the man drawled. "Got me twenty bucks on the Rangers."

"I'd like a little of that action." Dillon took another pull on his beer. "Can you hook me up?"

"Not me." When a commercial came on, the bartender dragged his eyes from the TV and inclined his head toward a man sitting at the opposite end of the bar. "Try Benny."

He was probably in his late fifties, Dillon thought. Short, thick glasses, blue plaid shirt. From his greased-down hair to his long face, everything about the man was thin, including the nose he stared down while he studied a racing form and scribbled in a little notebook.

"Thanks." Dillon dropped a few dollars on the counter, picked up his beer and moved beside the man.

"Hey, Benny, how's it going?"

Benny looked over his glasses. "Who the hell are you?"

"Name's Dillon Blackhawk."

"Good for you." Benny turned back to his racing form.

"I was looking for an old friend of my Daddy's from Wolf River," Dillon said. "Heard you were a friend of his and I thought maybe you could help me."

Benny looked up, then turned his beady gaze on

Dillon. "Do you see a goddamned Customer Service sign over my head? Go file a missing person's report with the sheriff."

"Well, now, isn't that a coincidence." Dillon leaned casually against the bar while he scanned the room. "My Daddy's friend used to be a sheriff. Sheriff Spencer Radick."

"Never heard of him."

It was the pause that gave Benny away. Only a millisecond, but just long enough for Dillon to know the man was lying. Dillon pulled out his wallet and slid two one-hundred-dollar bills onto the counter. Benny's eyes lit up.

"Radick, Radick." Benny pretended to be thinking hard, then he snatched it up and managed a smile. "Oh, yeah. Radick. *Long* time ago. Bastard died about four years ago, owed me ten G's."

"How'd he die?"

Another pause, Dillon noticed.

"Heart stopped." Benny snapped his fingers. "Just like that. Real tragic."

"Where's he buried?" Dillon asked and slid two more hundreds on the counter. "Just in case I decide to pay my respects."

"Do I look like a fucking mortician? How the hell would I know?" Sweat beaded on Benny's forehead. He licked his lips while he stared wishfully at the money, then he slammed his notebook closed and threw back the rest of his whiskey. "Been a real pleasure, but I think I ate something bad for lunch."

Dillon watched Benny disappear through a doorway leading to the restrooms. The man couldn't lie worth a damn, Dillon thought. No matter, it would be easier to deal with the bookie without an audience. Dillon turned back to the bartender. "There a back way outta here?"

Without taking his gaze off the television, the bartender walked over to Dillon, slipped the two hundreds off the bar and nodded. "Third door on the left."

Dillon got up slowly and walked to the restroom. No surprise, it was empty. He moved to the third door on the left, stood to the side as he opened it, then slowly glanced inside. The room was empty, but a door leading to the outside was ajar.

Dillon dashed out the door into the alley, sighed when he saw Benny scurrying away. *Looks like I'm going to have to exert myself,* Dillon thought with annoyance.

"Benny!"

"Nice talking to ya, Blackhawk!" Benny yelled over his shoulder, then threw his arm high over his head and made a rude gesture with his hand as he rounded the corner.

Now that was just plain rude. Dillon decided he

would have to teach the bookie a few manners when he caught up with him.

What the hell?

Dillon was halfway down the alley when Benny suddenly reappeared. His hands stretched out in front of him, he walked slowly backward.

A moment later, teeth bared, eyes narrowed and locked on Benny, Bowie came around the corner. Rebecca followed closely behind.

I'll be a son of a bitch.

"Good dog, good dog," Benny murmured over and over, keeping his arms out in front of him.

Growling fiercely, Bowie backed the man toward Dillon. Enjoying the show, Dillon folded his arms and leaned against the building. Later, Dillon told himself, he'd have to remember to thank them both.

Dillon met Rebecca's gaze. One corner of her pretty mouth curved up. "You told us to take a walk."

Sweat dripping down his face, Benny glanced frantically at Rebecca. "Lady, call your fucking mutt off."

"Actually, it's not my mutt." Rebecca nodded at Dillon. "It's his."

Benny looked over his shoulder at Dillon, swore, then smiled weakly and raised his shoulders in a friendly shrug. "Hey, no hard feelings, Blackhawk. You know how it is. Spence is an old friend and a good client. I can't rat him out."

"Fine." Dillon noticed the notebook Benny had shoved under the belt of his pants. "Just give me your book and I'll find him myself."

Benny clutched his notebook as if it were the Holy Grail. The sudden movement made Bowie lunge and snap at the man. Eyes wide, Benny shrieked.

"Call him off, call him off," Benny pleaded.

Dillon wasn't in that big a hurry he couldn't enjoy the moment and let Benny sweat a little more. "I'll call him off when you tell us where Radick is."

"Couple miles out of town," Benny said in a rush. "I'll give you directions."

"Tell you what." Dillon pushed away from the building. "I'll call the dog off, and you take us to Radick."

Benny licked his lips, glanced nervously back and forth between Dillon and the snarling dog. Bowie crouched lower and inched closer.

"Okay, okay, okay," Benny whimpered. "Just call him off."

"Bowie, off!" Dillon commanded the dog, who instantly backed away.

Benny closed his eyes and whispered a mixture of swear words and a prayer. His hand shaking, he wiped at the sweat on his brow, then opened his eyes again and looked at Rebecca. "Who the hell are you?"

"You're on a need-to-know basis right now, Benny." Dillon snapped a finger and Bowie came over to him. "Let's take a ride."

The pain woke her.

Like the others, the contraction started low, then stretched tighter and tighter across her belly. Teresa arched her neck on a soft moan, kept her eyes focused on the light overhead and forced herself to concentrate on her breathing. Slow, not too deep. Her stomach hardened, squeezed like a vise, then ever-so-gradually eased its steel-like grip.

Closing her eyes, she collapsed back onto the bed. Since her water had broke, the contractions had steadily increased in frequency and intensity. Without a clock, she wasn't certain exactly how close they were, though she'd guess four or five minutes. She'd dozed off and on, drifted in and out. Her world existed only within her body. No sense of time, or even place.

"You're doing wonderful, Teresa."

Teresa opened her eyes and glanced at Elena, who'd been by her side most of the day. "How much longer?"

Elena smiled. "Every woman is different. You're only dilated to five, so my guess is maybe another three or four hours."

A lifetime, Teresa thought. She wanted to hold

her baby now. Wanted to see her child take his or her first breath, hear their first cry.

"Is my baby all right?" Teresa asked. She knew one of the machines she was hooked up to monitored her baby's heartbeat, but there was no sound.

"Your baby is fine," the nurse reassured her. "You need to relax and stop worrying, honey. Didn't I tell you that we'd take good care of you and your baby?"

Teresa nodded. "You've been so kind."

"You'll be cursing me in a little while." Elena squeezed Teresa's hand. "But it will all be worth it."

"I know." Teresa smiled at the woman, then sucked in a breath when the next contraction started to tighten.

I know...I know...I know...

The old farmhouse and barn sat in a grove of cypress about a mile off the highway. Except for the peeling white paint, torn screens on the windows and several rusting pickups in the dirt yard, the place wasn't so bad, Rebecca thought. Nothing a bulldozer or several sticks of dynamite couldn't fix.

With Bowie on the seat beside her, Rebecca sat behind Benny, who'd kept one nervous eye on the dog since they'd all climbed in Dillon's truck. The one time he'd gestured for Dillon to turn, Bowie had growled and snapped, and Benny had been careful to give only verbal directions after that.

It had been a lucky break she'd gotten tired of waiting in the truck after Dillon had gone in the bar. Bowie had been anxious to stretch his legs and they'd only been out of the truck a couple of minutes when the man had come running around the corner and bumped into her.

Bowie hadn't liked that one little bit.

If Rebecca hadn't heard Benny use Dillon's name, then heard Dillon yell, she would have called the dog off. Having been on the wrong side of Bowie before, Rebecca had almost felt sorry for the bookie.

"He's home." Benny started to raise his hand and point, then quickly pulled it back when Bowie softly growled. Benny nodded at an old, dusty white Buick. "That's his car."

"Is he the friendly type?" Dillon parked beside the Buick and cut the engine.

"Friendly as you," Benny said sarcastically, then gulped when Dillon opened the lid on the center console and pulled out a hand gun.

Rebecca's heart leaped upward at the sight of the gun. It wasn't as if she'd never seen one before, or even held one. She had. Her stepfather had owned several for what he considered recreation, and Sean had a license to carry one on his planes. But something told her that Dillon's not only wasn't recreational, it probably wasn't licensed, either.

"Whadaya gonna do with that?" Benny asked, his eyes bulging.

Dillon slide a glance at Benny, then stepped out of the truck and shoved the gun into the waistband of his jeans under his T-shirt. "I just want information, that's all. Let's go."

A hot wind picked up the ends of Rebecca's hair as she and Bowie followed behind Dillon and Benny. Thunder rumbled in the distance. She tried to see beyond the dark windows, wondered if Radick was standing behind one of them, watching. Adrenaline pumped through her blood, kicked her heart into high gear.

Benny knocked loudly on the front door, then stood back and yelled, "Spence! It's Benny."

No answer.

Benny knocked again, then shouted, "Hey, Spence, I'm comin' in."

Still no answer.

Dillon pulled out the gun and held it to his side, then turned the knob and toed open the door. Other than a squeak from rusty hinges, it was absolutely quiet.

Too quiet.

Rebecca's pulse raced. Dillon motioned for Benny to go inside. "Call him again."

"Spence!" Nervous, Benny's voice cracked. He stuck his head in first, looked around, then moved through the door. "You here?"

The floorboards creaked when Benny and Dillon stepped inside. Wiping her sweat-dampened palms on her jeans, Rebecca followed.

The drapes were closed and it took a moment for her eyes to adjust to the dim light inside. The house was hot and stuffy, the air stale.

"He might be out in the barn," Benny said, glancing around. "Maybe I should go check."

"Maybe you should stay right here." Dillon looked inside the small kitchen, then nodded toward a hallway. "What's back there?"

"Two bedrooms and a bathroom."

"Open the doors."

"Me?" Benny's eyes nearly popped out of his head. "You got the gun."

"A man won't shoot his own bookie unless he owes him a lot of money," Dillon said. "Does he owe you a lot of money?"

Benny looked anxiously from the gun to Bowie, then back at the hallway. Mumbling something rude under his breath, Benny moved cautiously into the hall. Dillon followed.

"Just me, Spence." Benny opened the first closed door. He looked inside, then released the breath he'd been holding. He moved to the second bedroom, opened that door and once again heaved a sigh of relief.

"Just the bathroom in here," Benny said, turning the knob. The door creaked open. Benny's eyes widened and his jaw went slack. "Holy shit."

Rebecca couldn't see inside the bathroom past the two men, but she watched as Dillon pushed the door open and frowned.

"Looks like you were right, after all, Benny." Dillon lowered the gun in his hand. "He *is* dead."

Benny's face turned white as a sheet. "Holy shit," he repeated.

"Dead?" Breath held, Rebecca moved closer.

Dillon put up a hand to stop her. "You don't want to see this."

But it was too late. She was already at the door, could see the man lying in the free-standing bathtub. He had a peaceful look on his age-worn face, as if he were sleeping. Water the color of blood rose to his neck. One arm rested on the edge of the tub.

The wrist was slit open.

"Ohmigod." She turned quickly away and stepped back into the hall, struggled to find air to bring into her lungs.

"I just saw him yesterday," Benny murmured. "Jersey Boy paid off three big ones on a long shot. He was buying drinks for everyone at the bar."

"What time?" Dillon asked.

"Around noon, I guess, I'm not sure. He probably left around two or three." Benny shook his head in disbelief. "It don't make no sense he would do himself in. He had a sweet thing going."

Dillon shoved the gun back into the waistband of his jeans. "What sweet thing was that?"

Benny stared blankly at the man in the bathtub, then looked at Dillon. "Some guy sent regular checks. Big enough for Spence to live on and play the horses. He said he was set for life."

"He *was* set for life," Dillon looked at the man lying in the bathtub. "Someone just cut it short, is all."

"You mean this wasn't—" Benny furrowed his brow. "Somebody else did this?"

The house shook from another clap of thunder. Benny jumped and even Bowie whimpered. Rebecca laid her hand on the dog's head and the animal leaned into her.

"I don't want no part of this. I got me a reputation. People dying ain't good for business." Benny grabbed a hand towel off a rack and wiped at the bathroom doorknob, then went back to the other knobs he'd touched.

So much for loyalty and friendship, Rebecca thought in disgust.

"The checks he received." Dillon stepped out of the bathroom. "You know who sent them?"

"He never said." The color started to come back

into Benny's face. "He waved them around a few times when he wanted to place a bet. They were cashier checks."

"Did you see what bank they were drawn on?"

"Why the hell would I know something like—" Benny paused in his vigorous cleaning of a bedroom doorknob, then quickly resumed his work. "Maybe I do."

"No maybe." Dillon grabbed the man by the throat and shoved him against the wall. "You give me information and it better be right, or I promise you that you'll be the one taking a bath."

"All right, all right. You don't gotta get rough, dammit." Benny sagged backward when Dillon released him. "Hey, give me a break, pal. I just lost a buddy and a good customer. I'm grieving."

Scowling, Dillon pulled out his wallet, then crammed a fistful of money into the bookie's outstretched hand.

"Okay, it's coming back to me." Benny stuffed the money into his pants pocket. "One time, Spence kissed one of those checks and said if Corpus Christi was a woman, he'd fuck her."

Chapter 11

Fifty miles north of Abilene, the sky opened up.

Dillon pulled into a rundown motel called The Blue Haven Canyon Resort. Raindrops the size of quarters pelted the truck and bounced off the hard-packed dirt parking lot. Lightning flashed, and the air, charged with electricity, sizzled up his arms.

After they'd dropped Benny back off in Flat Falls, Dillon had headed south. Neither he nor Rebecca had spoken in the past hour. He'd simply driven, and she'd stared out the window.

"We'll stop here for the night."

As if she'd just realized he'd stopped the car, she turned and blinked. "What?"

"We can't keep driving in this." He cut the engine. "We'll weather it out here for the night, get a fresh start in the morning."

Both woman and dog hurried behind him to the front office of the motel, where a middle-aged woman with bags under her dull eyes glanced up from the soap opera she was watching. A sign sitting on the counter said Bernadette Is On Duty. The woman took one look at Bowie and frowned.

"No dogs."

"He's trained." He was too damn tired to argue the matter. Dillon dropped enough bills on the counter to make Bernadette's eyes brighten. The woman managed a smile as she heaved herself out of her chair.

"That'll buy you a suite," she said, as if an upgrade in this dump would make the exchange a fair deal.

"Number eight's the best we got." She plucked a key from the wall and slid it across the counter, then snatched up the cash. "Need anything else?"

"Food."

"I can have some pizza sent over." The woman stared hungrily at the wallet Dillon had shoved back into his jeans pocket. "You like pepperoni?"

"Fine." He dropped more money on the counter. "And a six-pack."

"You got it, mister." Bernadette, warmed by

Dillon's generosity, smiled at Rebecca. "Anything for you, honey?"

"Some extra towels, please."

The clerk stepped into a closet behind the counter, then came out with an armload of towels and handed them to Rebecca. "I'd have our bell cap help you with your luggage," the woman said, "but it's his day off."

They were all soaking wet by the time they made the short run to the room. Dillon closed the door behind them and slid the lock into place, then dropped his bag and Rebecca's suitcase on the sofa.

The "suite" had a small living area and a bedroom with a queen size bed. One TV in the living room. Dillon thought the place made the Mesa Motel look like the Waldorf, but the towels appeared clean enough and when he turned on the faucet in the bathroom, the water ran hot and clear.

He came back into the living area and found Rebecca kneeling on the floor, drying Bowie with a towel. The room smelled like wet dog and old carpet.

"Here." She tossed him a towel from the stack she'd set on a coffee table, then turned her head and grimaced when Bowie decided to shake his wet coat.

"I'll do that." He took the towel from her hand and helped her up. "Why don't you go rest until the food gets here."

When he held on to her hand, she looked up at him. "I suppose I could use a shower."

The bruise on her chin stood out against her pale skin. "Are you okay?"

She didn't answer for a long moment, just stared blankly at his chest, then finally said, "I've never seen anything like that before."

He had, only worse. Much worse.

"Don't think about it." He pulled her to him, rested his chin on top of her head. "It's done. Nothing can change it."

Lightning flashed, then a peal of thunder rumbled a second later. Bowie whined, then crawled under the coffee table.

"Waters did it, didn't he?" she whispered. "He knew we were getting close, so he had Radick killed. Made it look like a suicide, so no one would question it."

He smoothed his hands over her shoulders. "I shouldn't have let you see."

"I needed to." Cheek on his chest, she let out a long heavy breath. "I'm not as fragile as you think, Dillon."

"I don't think you're fragile."

There were tears in her eyes when she lifted her gaze. "You don't?"

Shaking his head, he smoothed the hair back from her face. "Most women would have crumpled under what you've been through. You did good, Rebecca."

She sighed, then dropped her forehead to his chest. "The man who attacked me killed Radick, didn't he?"

He wanted to pull her into the bedroom. Take the image out of her mind. Make her forget everything for at least a little while. But the timing was lousy, so it would have to wait.

He sighed, then dropped his arms and stepped back. "Go ahead and shower. We'll talk later."

She nodded, then picked up her suitcase and a couple more towels. She walked to the bedroom, turned at the doorway and looked at him. "Dillon?"

"Yeah?"

"I'm glad you have a gun."

The moan came from deep in her throat. Leaning forward, Teresa gripped the handrails, eyes squeezed shut, and pushed.

"That's a good one, honey." Elena stroked her arm. "You're doing wonderfully."

"Head's crowning," Dr. Wilson said from the foot of the bed. "Keep pushing, Teresa."

What other choice do I have? Teresa thought through her haze of pain. The pressure was like nothing she could have ever imagined, nothing anyone could have ever explained. Fingers wrapped tight around the handrails of the bed, she clenched her teeth and pushed as hard as she could.

Out of breath, sobbing, she fell back against the bed, heard Dr. Wilson mumble something to Elena about the IV. The nurse turned and picked up a syringe off a cart beside the doctor.

"This is just to calm you down a little and help you push," Elena said, injecting the syringe into the tube. "You might feel a little light-headed, but don't worry, you'll be fine."

"No," Teresa gasped, shaking her head. She didn't want drugs. She wanted to be wide awake, wanted to remember every precious moment of giving birth to her baby. She'd gotten through the worst without any drugs, she didn't want them now. "No drugs."

"Just a mild sedative," Dr. Wilson said. "Don't you worry. It won't have time to pass through your blood into the baby."

Unable to stop the fierce need to push, Teresa leaned forward again and gritted her teeth. She cried out at the pain squeezing her body.

"Head's out," Dr. Wilson said to Elena, who moved beside the doctor to assist. "Keep pushing, Teresa."

The doctor's voice suddenly sounded far away, the dim light in the room grew dimmer. The need to close her eyes overwhelmed her, but she refused to give into it. She held on, teeth tightly clenched, pushing, pushing, felt her baby slide from her body into the doctor's hands.

"What is it?" she asked, but realized her mouth hadn't moved and the question was only in her mind. She tried to lift her head, to see her baby, but she couldn't. What was happening to her?

She could feel the doctor still working between her legs, could hear voices, but couldn't understand the words. Helpless, Teresa watched Elena wrap a blanket around her tiny baby, then walk away.

Wait! Stop! Teresa tried to lift her arm, to call to the nurse, but she felt as if her body had turned to lead and her mind was floating away. *What's wrong?* she tried to ask, but it was impossible to form the words. A strange darkness slowly consumed her.

And in that darkness, Teresa felt a strong, uncontrollable urge to push.

The hot water felt good.

Hands flat on the ugly green and pink tile wall, Rebecca leaned forward in the large shower stall, head down and let the pulsating spray pummel her neck and shoulders. She'd been in a fog for the past few hours. Had felt disoriented, as if she were moving in slow motion.

She could still see Radick lying in that bathtub,

his wrists cut. So much blood. And yet, strangely, his face had a peaceful expression.

Shivering, she turned the water up hotter.

If the sight of Radick lying in a bathtub of blood had bothered Dillon, he hadn't shown it. She had the feeling it wasn't the first dead person he'd ever seen. Not just dead, she thought, closing her eyes.

Murdered.

If she hadn't fought off the man who had attacked her, is that how she would have ended up? In a bathtub of blood, wrists slit? *Poor woman,* they might have said. *So depressed over her mother's death, and the dreadful crime she'd committed.* Who would have questioned it?

Rebecca clenched her teeth. Sean and Melanie would have. In her heart, she knew they wouldn't have rested until the truth was known. To know that she had family, people who loved her, had never meant more to her than it did at this moment. Death did that, she realized. Made a person appreciate life all the more.

"Rebecca? You okay?"

She jumped at the sound of Dillon's voice in the bathroom, had to swallow the tightness in her throat before she could answer. "Yes."

"Food's here."

She couldn't see him through the thick glass of the shower door and the steam, but she could feel that he was still in the room. Knew that he stood no more than two feet from her. So close.

So far.

She pressed her back to the tile, felt her heart drum against her ribs. Through the shower door glass, his shadow appeared. He said nothing. Just stood there.

She couldn't breathe, couldn't move.

The click of the shower door echoed in the room. She lifted her eyes, watched his gaze rake hotly over her. Excitement shivered through her. A muscle jumped in Dillon's jaw when he lifted his gaze up again. His eyes glinted black.

He bent slowly, pulled off his boots. One by one, they dropped to the floor with a thud. He straightened, then tugged his T-shirt over his head. Rebecca's heart pounded wildly in her chest. Still, even at the sight of his broad, bare chest, even when he unsnapped his jeans and shoved them down, she kept her eyes on his. A voice in the back of her mind tried to tell her she should cover herself, that she should be embarrassed. But she wasn't. After all they'd been through, how could she be?

When he stepped into the shower and closed the door behind him, she raised her arms, then laid her palms flat on his chest, felt his strength, his virility.

Steam swirled around them, hot water sluiced over their bodies. She lifted her face to his.

He dropped his mouth on hers.

His kiss was every bit as exciting, as thrilling, as demanding as the first time. She slid her hands up his chest, wrapped her arms tightly around his neck. His tongue invaded, pillaged, and her senses reeled from the assault.

Madness. That's what this was. Complete madness.

The storm had moved inside these walls, she thought dimly. The lightning. The thunder. Right here. Inside her. Inside him.

He trailed kisses down her neck, slid his hand down her shoulder, then over her breast. His palms were rough on her sensitive skin. White-hot need shot through her. When his hand slid lower, then moved between her legs, she moaned.

"I need you," she gasped, then rose on her toes, slid her wet soft body against his wet hard body. His arousal pressed against her. "Inside me. Now, please, now."

He cupped her bottom in his big hands and lifted her. Instinctively, she wrapped her legs around his waist and rose over him, then slowly slid back down. He moaned when she took him inside her, then pressed her back against the tiled wall.

And then he began to move.

There was nothing gentle in his lovemaking. He thrust upward, hard, again and again, and she took him, again and again. Her body vibrated with need, her blood rushed through her veins, her heart pounded wildly. She clung desperately to him, dragged her nails over his shoulders, cried out when the climax slammed into her. While the shudders still coursed through her, she raked her hands through his damp hair and moved with him, felt him grow harder, larger. The wall shook with every lunge of his hips, but she held on. On a deep groan, his entire body tightened, then convulsed.

Panting, she dropped her head on his shoulder. He held her tightly, easily, as if she weighed no more than a pillow. A wet pillow, she thought with a smile.

When she slowly slid her legs down his, he bent and lowered her until her feet were flat on the shower floor. He took her hands in his and lifted them to his mouth, kissed each one. "You okay?"

Wanting to linger in the pleasure still shimmering through her, she simply nodded, then sighed and leaned back against the shower wall. Turning his back to the pulsing spray from the shower head, he shielded her from the strong blast of water, then lowered his head and pressed his mouth to hers.

His kiss was gentle this time. Slow and deep. His hands slid to her breasts, and his thumbs circled the hardened peaks. She arched into his palms, shocked at the desire that rose instantly at his touch. *So soon?* she thought in amazement. When his mouth lowered to her breasts, she drew in a breath at the hot need that speared through her. *Oh, yes.*

While his hands kneaded and caressed, he closed his mouth over her nipple and ran his tongue over the tight bead of her nipple. Pleasure shivered through her and she moaned, slid her hands over his scalp and down his neck. Her knees threatened to give out underneath her, so she steadied herself on his broad shoulders, felt the ripple of strong, hard muscle under her fingers.

His mouth was warm and wet, hungry. He moved to her other breast, nipping, tasting, then clamped onto the tight bud and sucked. She arched upward, felt the urgency rise sharply again. Already she ached to take him inside her again, needed him to ease the heavy throb of desire between her legs.

And then his mouth moved lower.

She opened her eyes, wanted to protest, but couldn't find the words or the strength. He kissed her belly, explored every slippery curve and hollow. His hands moved down her sides, over her hips, then one hand slipped between her thighs and spread her legs. He stroked her, with his fingers, then his mouth, his tongue. Her nails dug deeply into his shoulders. Sensations, as exquisite as they were fierce, flowed through her.

She was lost, desperate, her world spinning, in that place, that sweet, beautiful place, where pleasure and pain are one. He moved over her slowly, stroking, touching, until she thought she might scream.

She called out to him, murmured his name again and again, helpless to stop the shudder that broke, then rippled endlessly through her.

When he gathered her in his arms and held her close, she sighed. Definitely madness, she thought through the haze of desire still swirling in her blood.

What else could something like this possibly be?

Later, food forgotten, they lay under the covers, naked, wrapped in each other's arms. The storm still raged outside, but here, inside, with Bowie in the outer room and a gun in his bag beside the bed, Dillon let himself relax.

But then, after the past hour he'd spent making love with Rebecca, it would be damn hard not to be relaxed.

The physical release had been good for both of them. The strain of the past few days had wound them both up tight as a fist. He knew that sex had a way of balancing the mind and the body. The calm it brought, if only temporary, was as powerful a restorative as any medicine, modern or ancient.

It had been inevitable—predictable, even—they would sleep together. A natural joining of two people strongly attracted to each other.

What hadn't been inevitable, and certainly not predictable, had been his reaction when they did.

No woman had ever made him feel like Rebecca had. No woman had taken him to such depths of desperation, such heights of arousal. He'd never lost control before, never forgotten who he was, what he was doing. Once again, he'd stepped too close to a line he'd drawn long ago and he needed to remind himself to draw back.

And there was something else to be dealt with, something that needed to be said.

"Rebecca." He pressed his lips to her temple. "I didn't use protection."

She stilled, then sighed softly. "I—I realize that now. I wasn't thinking at the time."

"Neither one of us were." He rolled her to her back and gazed down at her. "You need to know I've never done that before."

"I've never done that before, either," she said awkwardly. "Forgotten, I mean. For that matter, I've only been with—"

She stopped, then bit her lip and glanced away, her cheeks darkening.

He shouldn't pursue the conversation, just the thought of who she had or hadn't been with before spurred up an emotion he'd rather not invoke—an emotion he'd never felt for any woman before.

But he couldn't seem to stop himself. He wanted to know. *Needed* to know. The wondering about it would be a distraction, and he certainly didn't need any more distractions than already faced them.

He reached out and slipped a finger under her chin, lifted her face. "Been with who?"

"I had a boyfriend in my junior year at college. We were always…both of us, very careful." She lifted her gaze. "I had other boyfriends, but there hasn't been anyone I—that I slept with."

In a way, he was glad. If she'd been a virgin, he'd have to deal with that. But other than the fact they'd established they were both healthy, there was still one other, very important issue. "Are you on the pill?"

"I—" She blinked. "No."

"All right." With his fingers, he combed her still damp hair back from her temples and pressed a kiss to her swollen lips. "We'll deal with that later, if we need to. Next time, we won't take any chances."

She didn't reply, or dispute that there would be a next time. They both knew there would.

The rain had eased some, and thunder still rattled the walls every few minutes. They'd stay here for the night, he'd already decided, but he hoped like hell they could get back on the road early tomorrow.

He had no intention of waiting around until Waters or one of his cronies sneaked up on them. Next time, Dillon told himself, he'd be ready.

"Why did you leave?" Rebecca asked, breaking the quiet that had settled around them.

He looked at her, realized she'd been watching him. "Leave?"

"Sixteen years ago." She traced his collarbone with her fingertips. "Why did you leave after you graduated high school and never go back?"

Her question made his pulse jump. He'd never discussed that with anyone before. Had never wanted to. Did he want to now?

He rolled away from her, then sat on the edge of the bed and stared into the shadows that had invaded the room.

"I'm sorry," she said softly. "It's none of my business."

For sixteen years, he'd forced that night from his mind. Had refused to let himself think about it. But it came rushing back to him now. Driving up to his house at midnight, the crunch of gravel under the tires of the brand new Porsche his father had given him for graduation. Every light in the house was on.

"I came home early from an all-night graduation party. They weren't expecting me."

"Dillon—"

"They were arguing upstairs, screaming at each
other." He'd had a couple of beers, but he'd been
more interested in driving than drinking that night,
so he'd come home. "I'd heard them argue before,
but nothing like this. Never with such venom and
such hatred."

"You don't have to tell me this," Rebecca whispered. But he did, he realized. For the first time in
his life, he needed to tell someone.

"I could barely understand what they were saying at first," he went on, "but then I realized my
mother wanted a divorce. My father refused to
give her one, told her that he'd tell me the truth if
she left him."

His mother's voice…*I hate you, I hate you*…the
sound of a fist breaking plaster. A floorboard had
creaked when he'd walked up the stairs. But his
parents hadn't heard it.

"She told him maybe it was time I knew the
truth, anyway, that I wasn't a child anymore. I was
a man. That only made my father more angry."
Glass breaking, his mother sobbing. "I'd never
heard my mother stand up to my father like that before. She told him that I had a right to know who
my real father was, and what did it matter, any-

way? She told him she knew he had a mistress, that he'd had one for years. She called him a phony and a hypocrite. He called her a whore. That's when I pushed their door open."

Dillon closed his eyes against the pain that shot through his chest. The shock on his mother's face, the anger on his father's, would always be etched in his brain.

He felt Rebecca's hand on his back, comforting, caring. It was almost more than he could bear. Lifting his head, he set his teeth and blew out a breath.

"I asked them who my father was," Dillon continued. "My mother was too stunned to speak. My father yelled at me, told me he was my goddamned father and no one else. All that mattered, he said, was that I wasn't some goddamned half-breed, that my blood wasn't tainted with white. When I looked at my mother, she cried, told me she was sorry. I just turned and walked back down the stairs."

"And that's when you left?" Rebecca moved closer, laid her cheek on his back.

He nodded. "My father caught up with me at the front door. Told me to go to my room. When I refused, he caught my jaw with his fist and I fell back against the wall. He stood over me, told me he'd raised me and I'd better damn well do what he said.

I straightened, then reached for the door knob. He hit me again and I heard my mother scream. When he reached for me a third time, I hit him back."

Dillon looked at his hand, realized that he'd made a fist, only the fist he saw had blood on it. His father's blood. He shook the image off, then loosened his fingers.

"I drove my car to the edge of town and left it there. Hitchhiked across the state, working on ranches and odd jobs here and there. Three months later I finally called. A stranger answered the phone, a housekeeper. She told me my mother had died of a heart attack three weeks earlier. I joined the army the next day."

"I'm so sorry," Rebecca whispered, then pressed her lips to his shoulder.

When he felt her hot tears slide down his back, he stood and yanked on his jeans, then dragged his hands through his hair and paced to the doorway. He needed distance, space.

God, he could barely breathe.

"Dammit, Rebecca, don't cry for me." He whirled back to face her. "I don't deserve it. I left her there with him. Walked out without even listening to whatever she might have told me. And then she died."

"And you blame yourself?"

"She stayed with my father—the man I thought

was my father—all those years because of me. When she needed me the most, I was too selfish, too angry, to stick around. Who the hell else would I blame?"

"Your mother made a choice." With the sheet covering her, Rebecca pulled her knees up and wrapped her arms around her legs. "You might not understand why now, maybe you never will, but you have to believe that she did what she thought was best."

"Is that what your mother did?"

He saw the hurt flare in Rebecca's eyes, felt it cut into him like a knife. Would he always bring pain to the people he cared about most?

Yes, the answer speared him. He would.

"I know my mother loved me," Rebecca said quietly, holding his gaze. "And I have no doubt your mother loved you. We can't change the past. Not five minutes ago, or twenty-four years ago. You're the one who said that to me, remember? It's what we do now, who we are from this moment on, that truly matters."

Naive, he thought. She was so damn naive. Everyone had to pay for their sins. It was the law of the universe. He'd denied it for the past sixteen years, had tried to run from it. But no more.

No more.

She raised a hand and held it out to him. "Come to bed, Dillon."

He stared at her, wanted her with a desperation that terrified him. His first thought was to walk away, to run.

No more.

Cursing her, cursing himself, he moved toward her.

Chapter 12

"So let's hear what my money bought me, Señor Worthington."

"Nothing but the best, Antonio, my friend."

Smiling, Leland leaned back in the chrome and leather desk chair in his office at home. On the computer monitor in front of him, he glanced at the photos and birth information he'd been e-mailed fifteen minutes ago.

"They were born an hour ago, the boy first. Five pounds, three ounces, twenty-two inches long." Leland looked at the second photo and stats. "The girl was two minutes later. Five pounds even, twenty-one inches long. No complications at all, both babies have a clean bill of health."

"I'm sure you won't mind if I have my own doctor present to examine them when we make the exchange," Antonio said. "Not that I don't trust you, Leland. But you know I'm a cautious man."

"Of course I don't mind. It's a healthy thing to be cautious." The preliminary examination and blood workup had already shown the twins to be in excellent health, but Leland understood Antonio's prudence. "If you are not completely satisfied, your money will be refunded and we will find a suitable home for the children elsewhere."

Leland wasn't worried. Not once had a baby ever been returned. Even the most demanding, uncompromising clients turned into weepy-eyed, sniveling masses of emotion when that little bundle of joy was placed in their arms.

And as far as babies went, this boy and girl were a fine-looking set of twins, Leland thought, studying the photos on the monitor. Probably the best he'd ever seen, especially for one hour old. They both had good color, the shape of their heads was nice and round, a nice shadowing of dark hair. Hell, if he liked kids, he'd be tempted to take them himself.

"Any distinguishing birthmarks?" Antonio asked.

"Not on my report." Leland skimmed through

all the medical information he'd been sent, but didn't see any mention of birthmarks. "I'll double check and let you know."

"Will the mother be a problem?"

"No." The mother was still unconscious, Leland knew, and would be for several hours yet. Even after she woke up, she'd be kept on drugs until long after the babies were delivered, then sent on her way with a nice, fat check. "You don't need to worry yourself about her."

"Like I said, I'm a cautious man." Antonio's tone turned harsh. "I would want nothing that could be traced back to me, or to you. Do you understand?"

"Completely," Leland replied. "I assure you, Señor Medini, if there is the slightest hint of a problem, I will handle it."

A Jane Doe found dead of an overdose in an alley. There'd be an investigation, but without family or friends looking for her, it would take the authorities months to ID her.

But it didn't have to be that way, Leland thought. As long as the woman—he glanced at the report—Teresa Bellochio, didn't raise a stink, there was no reason to harm her. Considering the size of the check he'd already drawn up for her, he was certain the Bellochio woman would be busy with some therapeutic shopping in a day or two.

"Where and when would you like us to make delivery?" Leland asked.

"My wife and I will check into the Marriott on Wednesday morning." Antonio put his hand over the phone and said something to his wife, then removed his hand. "We will need a little time to prepare. Three o'clock should be good for us."

Leland gritted his teeth. Dammit. It was only Monday. He'd hoped to unload the babies in the morning, especially now that he'd changed his plans and was leaving Thursday instead of Friday.

"Three o'clock, Wednesday, then." Leland put a smile in his voice. *"Ciao."*

What the hell, Leland sighed when he hung up the phone. He supposed it didn't really matter if the delivery was Tuesday or Wednesday. The only person who could have pointed a finger at him was floating in a bathtub of his own blood.

And by this time tomorrow, Leland thought, glancing at his Rolex, Dillon Blackhawk and the Blake woman would be just as dead as Spencer Radick.

Dillon woke to the sound of rain falling lightly outside the motel window. The worst of the storm had seemed to pass during the night, all that was left now was a dull drizzle. He glanced at the clock on the nightstand. It was almost seven.

Rebecca lay sleeping in the crook of his arm, one arm draped across his stomach, one leg wrapped around his thigh. Her hair tumbled across his chest; he resisted the urge to run his fingers through the soft, shiny curls.

Instead, he simply watched her.

Her chest rose and fell slowly, her breath shimmered across his belly like a silk scarf. The beat of her heart, steady and sure, vibrated through him.

He'd never known such contentment. Had never lost himself so completely, so carelessly. Though that matter still concerned him, he saw no reason to dwell on it at the moment. What had happened, happened, and couldn't be changed now.

She'd said that to him last night. *We can't change the past. Not five minutes ago, or twenty-four years. It's what we do now, from this moment on, that matters.*

If only life were that simple, he thought.

The tips of her fingers twitched, and she stirred, murmuring softly. Something in his chest shifted, an unfamiliar need, a warmth, that made him frown. He told himself it was the situation, not the woman, that evoked the emotion. The pleasure they shared had been as unique as the circumstances that had brought them together. Once there was closure on the past, she would go back to Boston. Back to her family, her teaching. Her life. He would go back to…what?

Hell, he didn't know.

She moved against him, stretching as she woke. His blood heated; his heart quickened. Need, like a fist, gripped hold of him. Even after a night of making love, he wanted her again. He wanted her desperately. He wanted her now.

When he yanked her on top of him, her eyes popped open and she gasped. Chestnut curls danced around her startled face, spilled down her soft shoulders. He grabbed a handful of her thick hair at the same time he slammed his mouth up against hers.

"Wait." She yanked her head back, sucking in air, and looked down at him. Her eyes, sleepy blue, turned to blue fire.

And then her hands were in his hair, and her mouth on his.

It shouldn't be like this, he thought. Not after last night. He shouldn't want her this bad, shouldn't ache. Shouldn't hunger.

But, God help him, he did.

With one hand still in her hair, he reached down into his duffel bag and fumbled until he felt the foil packet, fumbled and swore while she moved down his chest like a firestorm. He moaned when her tongue slid down his belly, then sucked in a breath when she slid lower still.

He clenched his teeth, groaned when she

slowly, tentatively, took in the hot, thick heat of him. His fist tightened in her hair and he rocked his hips while she moved over him. Desire blinded him to everything but the exquisite sensations pounding at him.

He couldn't stand it, thought he might die if he wasn't inside her. He reared up, then rolled her to her back, spread her legs with his knee and thrust deep inside her. She arched upward on a moan, reached up to him. He wrapped his hands around her wrists and slid her arms over her head, pinned her against the mattress. Her eyes, heavy with need and lust, opened and she smiled, rocked her hips against his.

They strained against each other, both of them gasping, rushing recklessly, then shattered together, an explosion of white light, then shimmering sparkles. Was this what it felt like to die? he wondered, or to be born?

Both, he decided and pulled her close.

The fog trapped her.

Teresa struggled against it, willed her eyes to open, her arm to move, but there seemed to be no connection between her brain and her body. Confused, frightened, she struggled through the thick haze that enveloped her.

Where am I?

She heard sounds. A deep hum. A squeak of rubber soles on a tile floor and the beep of a machine. She realized the deep hum was a man's voice.

"Teresa, can you hear me?"

Her eyelids felt like lead, but slowly she opened them, saw a man standing on one side of the bed and a woman on the other. So familiar…

Dr. Wilson, she realized. And Elena. Why were they looking at her like that?

"Awake at nine-thirteen," the doctor said, glancing at his watch. "Make a note of that."

It came rushing back to her. The pushing, giving birth, the nurse wrapping a blanket around her tiny baby, then the blackness. Complete and utter blackness.

Panic ripped through her and her gaze darted around the room. *Dear God. Where is my baby?*

"My baby," she managed, but the words were barely a whisper. Her throat was so dry.

Elena stroked her arm gently. "Why don't you rest for a while, Teresa?"

"No." She tried to push herself up on her elbows, but her arms refused to move. "My baby."

"There was a complication." Dr. Wilson laid his hand on hers. His fingers were cold, his palm damp. "I'm so sorry to tell you that there were complications. Your child didn't make it."

Teresa closed her eyes. She could feel her heart

pounding against her ribs, inside her head. "I don't understand."

"The heart was underdeveloped. There was nothing we could do." Dr. Wilson patted her hand. "I'm so sorry."

Sorry? He was *sorry?*

No, no, no! This wasn't happening. It couldn't be. Her baby had been healthy. She'd never even taken an aspirin while she'd been pregnant. The doctor had told her everything was fine, that her baby was fine. *I'm asleep,* Teresa thought frantically. This was a nightmare. A horrible, horrible nightmare. It *had* to be.

Please, God, let me wake up.

She opened her eyes, saw the solemn, sympathetic expressions on the doctor's and nurse's faces.

It was true. Dear God, it was true.

The sob rose from her chest, sucking the breath from her. Pain, so sharp, so intense, that she was certain she would die from it.

And as the tears slid down her cheeks, she prayed to God she would.

They ate lunch on the covered patio of a busy truck stop coffee shop outside of Austin. Cool, overhead misters and tall glasses of ice water offered relief from the miserable midday heat. Under the wooden table, Bowie lay at Rebecca's feet, intently watching the other diners on the open patio. The scent of grease and barbecue sauce hung heavy in the humid air, and the ground rumbled from the wheels of trucks pulling in and out of the huge parking lot.

It felt safe, Rebecca realized, to be in a crowded, public place. It felt safe to be with Dillon.

While she nibbled on her chicken salad, she watched him take a healthy bite of the roast beef sandwich he'd ordered, then crunch into a slice of pickle. There had been very little talk between them since they'd left the motel this morning.

But then, there'd been little talk between them last night, either.

She'd never experienced anything like the night she'd just shared with Dillon. Couldn't have possibly imagined that kind of passion existed. Even now, just thinking about it, made her breasts ache, her skin tingle. She'd been positively overwhelmed by the intensity, the power. The uninhibited, raw need.

Perhaps it was the situation, she reasoned. Everything that had happened over the past few days. The danger, the tension. Death. All of those things heightened a person's senses, made life seem more precious, more urgent.

And yet, for her, it was more. She was certain

of it. More than the attraction, more than the physical joining. It hardly seemed possible, but in her heart, she knew it was true.

She was in love.

She knew better than to think about it, knew better than to let herself believe he could love her back. But that didn't—couldn't—stop her feelings. He wanted her, and for now, for whatever time they had together, that would have to be enough.

A soft bark under the table rescued Rebecca from her unwanted thoughts. Bowie had sat abruptly, his ears pricked forward, and stared intently across the patio. Rebecca followed the direction of the dog's gaze and spotted the big, fat tabby cat sitting on the edge of the patio. The cat had spotted Bowie, as well, and stared back with a bored expression on its whiskered face.

"Bowie," Dillon warned. "Stay."

Bowie obeyed, but never took his eyes off the cat.

"He doesn't like cats?" Rebecca asked, watching the tabby flick its tail.

"I'm not sure." Dillon picked up his water and drained the glass. The ice clinked when he set it back down. "I just found him four months ago."

"You found him?"

"We'd had reports of some drifters living in a van close to an electrical shed a few miles from the refinery. I was sent to check it out," Dillon said, glancing down at the dog. "Whoever had been there had already moved on and left piles of flattened cardboard and trash behind. I was getting some gloves and a garbage bag to clean up the mess when I saw some movement under the trash, then noticed a dog's paw sticking out."

Rebecca frowned. "Someone left their dog under a pile of trash?"

Dillon nodded. "He was barely alive. Had a bullet hole in his hind quarter."

"Ohmigod." She sucked in a breath, shook her head. "Why would anyone do such a horrible thing?"

"Who knows?" he said with a shrug. "It might have been an accident, or maybe they just decided they didn't want a dog anymore. Or maybe they thought it would be fun to have a little shooting practice."

The thought of it made her stomach clench. She set her fork down, waited a moment for the sickening anger to ease. "What happened?"

"I got him in my truck and took him to a vet in town. The doc said I should put him down, but I said patch him up and I took him home. I thought I'd lost him a few times in the first three days, then he turned a corner."

"That's why he ran when you brought that bottle out of the cupboard." Rebecca reached out and touched Bowie's large head, but the dog still had his eyes trained on the cat. "He knew firsthand how bad it is."

Dillon smiled. "By the end of the week, he was eating and getting around by himself. Within three weeks, you'd never know he'd been sick."

"So you know nothing about him?" Rebecca asked.

"Vet says he's about three years old, probably a mix of shepherd and black lab." Dillon tore off a piece of his sandwich and handed it to Bowie. The dog gulped it down, but didn't lose sight of his prey. "I was assigned to a K-9 unit in the army for a short while, so I knew a little about working with dogs. He's one of the smartest I've ever seen. Sometimes I'm not sure if I trained him, or him, me, but it seems to have worked out okay."

Rebecca tried to imagine what kind of person would hurt an animal like that and leave it for dead, but she simply couldn't. But then the image of Spencer Radick lying in the bathtub flashed in her mind, and she knew firsthand there were all kinds of people in the world. Some of them did horrible, terrible things.

When the cat rose, arching its graceful, feline back, then turned with a flick of its tail, Bowie shivered with anticipation and whimpered while the tabby strolled away.

"Not this time, pal." Dillon ruffled the dog's head, then looked at Rebecca. "You finished?"

She looked at her half-eaten salad, then pushed it away. She no longer had any interest in food.

While Dillon paid the check, Rebecca waited with Bowie in front of the diner. Row after row of huge trucks and trailers were parked between the restaurant and the busy gas station next door. Two truckers wearing white T-shirts and baseball caps came out of the restaurant, talking about the time they'd lost from last night's storm.

Though they weren't even close, Bowie growled deep in his throat, then *woofed* softly when the men walked to their trucks. Rebecca laid a hand on the dog's head to calm him. It was certainly easy to understand why the animal was so distrusting of strangers. She was feeling more than a little skittish herself these days.

"We should make Corpus Christi before dark," Dillon said when they were back in the truck and heading south on the interstate.

"It's a big city," Rebecca said with a sigh. "How will we find him?"

"Most likely, he's still practicing law of some kind, though not under the same name. He'd be much too careful for that. But one way or the other, sooner or later, we'll find him."

Why did she feel such a strong sense that it had

to be sooner, or they wouldn't find him at all? It didn't make sense after twenty-four years, that a day, or week, would make a difference.

But it did. She felt a strange, overwhelming and unreasonable sense of doom that if they didn't find him immediately, something bad was going to happen.

The road stretched out before them like a shimmering asphalt snake. Dillon passed a couple of big rigs, who gave him a friendly honk and waved as he passed, but the road wasn't busy today. A sign on the side of the highway indicated a curve and downgrade, warning large trucks to slow down. Dillon backed off his speed through the curve, then hit the cruise control.

Between the lack of sleep and the food she'd just eaten, Rebecca felt her eyelids grow heavy. She fought against it, but the monotony of the empty highway and sparse scenery had her eyes closing.

"Rebecca," Dillon said sharply. "Wake up."

"Sorry." Yawning, she forced her eyes open. But something in his tone, the tight set of his jaw, dissipated her exhaustion. She straightened, then narrowed her eyes. "What's wrong?"

"Look behind us."

She turned, saw the shiny blue big rig barreling straight at them.

Chapter 13

In the rear view mirror, Dillon watched the big rig bear down on them. It made no attempt to slow down, did not even use its horn to warn of a problem. Like a huge blue dragon, it flew at them, chrome teeth open wide, belching black smoke, closing the distance between them. Because they were on a downgrade, the distance closed fast.

Dammit!

"What's happening?" Eyes wide, Rebecca looked back at him.

"We got company." Dillon hit the gas and the truck responded with a surge of power, but he knew it wouldn't be enough to outrun the eighteen-wheeler.

Dillon calculated their chances of survival if he veered off the highway. The shoulder angled sharply down. At the speed they were traveling, the odds were high they would flip and roll. Not an option, he decided. But with the blue behemoth on his butt, he couldn't slow down to pull off, either.

"He's getting closer." Panic edged Rebecca's voice. She held on to the shoulder strap of her seat belt, sucked in a breath. "Oh, God, he's going to hit us."

"That's the idea." Dillon floored the accelerator. "Hang on."

Rebecca cried out and grabbed hold of the door handle as the big rig's chrome bumper kissed the pickup's fender. With a yelp, Bowie flew off the back seat onto the floor.

"Take the wheel," Dillon yelled at Rebecca.

"What!" She looked at him as if he'd lost his mind.

"Take the wheel," he repeated. He set the cruise control, then opened the center console and pulled out his gun. "Just hold it steady."

"Dillon, I can't—"

"Now, dammit!" He unbuckled his seat belt. "Just do it!"

She grabbed the wheel, and he scrambled into the back seat, then opened the back window. When Dillon stuck his arm out and took aim, the driver of the rig pulled up a gun of his own and fired through his windshield. Rebecca gasped when the first bullet shattered the side mirror, then screamed when the second bullet ripped through the cab of the truck.

"Slide over and get behind the wheel," Dillon shouted at Rebecca, hoped she could hear him over the roar of the big rig behind them.

Dillon held his gaze steady, his arm straight and fired, swore hotly when he missed his target. He ignored the bullet that *pinged* somewhere close to his head. *Focus, focus…* He fired again.

Bingo.

Tread ripped like paper off the tire Dillon shot. The eighteen-wheeler went into a screeching skid across the road. The driver made a desperate attempt to correct the out of control rig, but when the tires hit the shoulder, there was nothing he could do. Truck and trailer jackknifed and flipped, then slid across the hard dirt.

"Payback's a bitch, ain't it, buddy?" Dillon shouted out the back of the truck, then looked at Rebecca. "Turn around."

"What?" She stared at him as if he were crazy. "He has a gun."

"So do I, sweetheart."

While Dillon ducked back into the cab, Rebecca slowed the truck, then made a U-turn and drove back to the big rig. It lay crumpled on the side of the road like a downed beast, belly exposed. Dust swirled around the wreckage. Metal creaked and groaned.

"Stay here," he commanded.

"You better be talking to Bowie," she said, opening the driver's door, then slid out on obviously shaky legs. He didn't have time to argue with her, knew it probably wouldn't do any good if he did. He quickly glanced to the left, then the right. The highway was deserted, but it wouldn't be for long. With Rebecca close on his heels, he sprinted across the road to the overturned rig, his gun lifted, his finger taut on the trigger.

Eyes trained on the cab, Dillon approached cautiously. He couldn't see the driver through the cracked windshield. Black smoke billowed out of the engine; the heavy scent of diesel filled the hot air. Adrenaline pumping, Dillon moved closer, his gaze locked on the cab.

No movement.

Flames crackled and rose through the thick smoke. Dillon motioned for Rebecca to get back, then he crouched, circled the cab and leaped up on the tangled trailer. Metal crunched under his boots as he inched closer to the cab. He reached around and flipped open the driver's door, then ducked back, expecting a bullet to fly by.

Nothing.

He raised his gun, inhaled sharply, then quickly glanced inside.

A man lay against the passenger door, one leg twisted backward, obviously broken. Blood streamed from a wound on his head. He lay perfectly still.

His gun still primed, Dillon crawled down into the cab, reached out a hand and touched it to the man's neck. No pulse. Dillon lifted the man's right hand and examined it.

No question about it, this was their man. Holding his breath against the increasing smoke, Dillon searched the man and retrieved a wallet from his back pocket. He shoved it in the waistband of his jeans, then spotted a sports bag on the floor and grabbed that, too.

"Dillon!" Rebecca yelled. "The cab's on fire! Get out of there!"

When he climbed out of the cab and jumped down, Rebecca rushed to him. He kept moving, grabbed her arm and pulled her with him as he sprinted back to the truck. "We've got to get out of here before anyone shows up."

"But we need him," Rebecca insisted, looking

back over her shoulder. "He can tell us where Waters is."

"He won't be telling anyone anything," Dillon said tightly. "Come on."

Bowie greeted them with a shrill bark when they jumped back into the truck. Dillon tossed the bag into the front seat, then got behind the wheel and punched the accelerator, throwing dirt and dust off the back tires as they sped off.

The entire ordeal, from the first sight of the big rig coming up on them until now, couldn't have been more than six or seven minutes.

Behind them, thick, black smoke billowed upward. Panting, Rebecca closed her eyes and laid her head back against the seat. "Are you sure it was him?"

"His right hand had a bite mark."

She opened her eyes, then sighed heavily and stared at the shimmering asphalt ahead. "So we're back to square one?"

"Not necessarily." Dillon made a point to keep his speed close to the limit. The last thing they needed was to get stopped by a trooper or sheriff. He pulled the wallet out of his waistband and tossed it to her. "I got this and his travel bag."

Her hands trembled as she opened the wallet. "Lawrence Gibson," she read the driver's license. "There's an address in Oklahoma."

"We'll check it out, but it will most likely be phony. What else?"

"Two credit cards, five hundred dollars, mostly twenties."

"That's it?"

She searched every pocket, then shook her head. "That's it."

"Dammit." He swiped the sweat on his forehead with the back of his hand, came away with soot on his knuckles. "Check the bag."

She lifted the black sports bag from the floor of the truck, hesitated, then drew in a deep breath and zipped it open. "Two T-shirts, one white button up shirt, socks."

When she stilled and her face paled, Dillon glanced into the bag and saw what she was looking at.

Latex gloves.

"He's dead, Rebecca," Dillon said quietly. "He can't hurt you anymore."

"I know."

When she still didn't move, he reached across the seat. "I'll do it."

"No." She held on to the bag. "I'm fine."

"Rebecca—"

"I'm fine." Color came back into her cheeks, and determination flared in her eyes. "I am."

She rooted through the bag again. "Small bag of toiletries, pack of cigarettes—"

Rebecca gasped when something buzzed inside the bag. Her fingers shook as she reached into a side pocket and pulled out a flip cell phone.

"Open it." Dillon stared at the phone. "But don't answer it."

She flicked open the case. "There's a number on the display."

"Let me see it." Dillon memorized the number when Rebecca held it out to him, then nodded. "You got a pen in your purse?"

The phone went silent.

"No message left," she said. Reaching into her purse, she pulled out a pen and handed it to Dillon.

He wrote the number on the inside of his palm, then spotted the highway patrol car coming at them. He tensed, kept his gaze on the car until he couldn't see it in his rear view mirror any longer, then exhaled the breath he'd been holding. In about two minutes, the officer would come across the wreckage and all hell would break loose.

"Will they be looking for us?" Worry furrowed Rebecca's brow as she stared at the highway behind them.

"There were no witnesses, plus the rig was most likely stolen back at the truck stop. That's what they'll investigate for now."

He glanced at the number he'd written on his palm, then pulled a cell phone out of the front pocket of his jeans and dialed. "Alpha Dog 82347," he said when a computer clicked on at the other end of the line.

A moment later, a familiar voice came on the phone. "Hey, Blackhawk, don't hear from you for two years and now you're a regular chatterbox."

Dillon might have made a crude reply, but knew that Rebecca was watching him and listening. He would have rather made the call privately, but he needed information and it couldn't wait.

"I need a cell phone trace." He read the numbers off that he'd written down. "Get back to me soon as you can. Yeah, I know. I owe you."

When he hung up, Rebecca stared at him, a mixture of curiosity and bewilderment. "What exactly did you do in the army?" she asked cautiously.

For a long moment, he didn't answer, then he just shook his head. "You don't want to know."

"No," she said with a sigh and turned her gaze back to the road ahead of them. "I suppose I don't."

The old man refused to leave.

The first time Teresa saw him, he stood silently in the corner of the dimly lit hospital room. Hair the color of fresh snow hung past his shoulders, framed a dark face deeply etched from years. He wore a heavily beaded buckskin jacket and leggings. His arms were folded over his broad chest, and though she couldn't see his eyes, she knew he watched.

Teresa knew the man wasn't really there, knew he was a result of the drugs Dr. Wilson had given her. But strangely, even though he never spoke or moved, she found comfort in his presence.

Through the haze still clouding her vision, she looked at him now, wondered if maybe he'd come to guide her to the other side. She hoped he had. Only there could she be with her precious Cade.

An anomaly, the doctor had called her son. *Condition nonconducive to life.*

Dr. Wilson had made all the necessary arrangements for her, to make it easier for her, he had told her, but Teresa wished she could have at least held her son once, kissed his tiny forehead and said goodbye. She closed her eyes against the pain that sliced through her chest. It simply wasn't possible to bear sorrow this intense, she thought.

"Teresa."

She heard the voice, opened her eyes slowly, hoping it was the old man, praying that he'd finally stepped forward to take her. But when the form beside the bed took shape, it was Dr. Wilson. Disappointment flooded through her.

"Wake up, Teresa." The doctor smiled at her. "How are you feeling, dear?"

How am I feeling? If she hadn't been so tired, so numb with grief, the question would have angered her. But that was wrong, she knew. She didn't blame the doctor. She was certain he'd done all he could do to save her baby. He was a doctor, wasn't he?

"I'm all right," she lied, though the words came out slurred on her thick tongue.

He placed a stethoscope on her chest and listened. "I'm going to take your IV out now, and later, if you're up to it, Elena will help you take a shower. You didn't tear with your delivery, so without stitches, you'll be able to walk without any pain."

Without pain? A bubble of hysteria formed in her throat. Didn't he know? She would always have pain. *Forever.*

"Thank you," she said quietly, barely felt it when the doctor slid the IV out of her arm, then cleaned and bandaged the tiny wound.

"I'm going to give you something to rest now." Dr. Wilson pulled a tiny white envelope from his white coat. "When you wake up later, we'll talk about getting you some help when you go home."

I don't have a home, she thought, but even that didn't matter to her now. She welcomed sleep. Anything to shut off the feeling.

The doctor placed two small yellow pills into her mouth, then pressed a glass of water in her hand. She struggled to lift her heavy arm, but with the doctor's help, managed to raise the glass to her lips.

A movement from the corner caught her attention. The old man again. He shook his head. *I know you aren't really there,* she told herself, but she felt his intense gaze on her. Warning her? Teresa looked back at the doctor, who smiled at her.

She sipped the water and swallowed.

"That's a good girl," he said, taking the glass from her. "You rest now."

The doctor left the room and Teresa closed her eyes. She heard the heavy beat of her heart, steady, sure. Lifting her arm, she brought her hand to her mouth.

And spit out the pills.

When she opened her eyes again, she glanced back at the corner.

The old man nodded.

"What do you mean, there's been a change of plans?"

Leland had been shredding some of the more sensitive documents in his office and clearing out his desk when his cell phone had rung. He'd hoped it would be Edmunds, but it had been Antonio instead.

"I want you there tomorrow when we make the exchange," Antonio said on the other end of the line.

"That's really not necessary, Antonio." Though he kept his voice calm and reassuring, annoyance rumbled in his gut. "As we discussed, the delivering doctor and nurse will handle the exchange."

"I don't need you to tell me what we discussed." Antonio's voice had a deadly tone to it, then he chuckled softly. "The cigars you sent are meant to be shared, my friend. We will smoke one together, to celebrate both our good fortunes, yes?"

Leland hadn't gotten as far in life as he had by being stupid. Antonio Medini was not a man anyone said no to, unless they wanted to end up dead or with missing body parts. Or both.

Dammit! Leland ground his teeth. It was too late to back out, even if Medini was suddenly changing things. Antonio made the rules, and broke them if he so saw fit. Leland knew there wasn't a damn thing he could do about it. There wouldn't be a place on this earth he could hide if he pissed off Medini.

Leland sighed. So he would leave a couple of hours later than he planned. What the hell. What difference would a couple of hours make, anyway?

"I'll bring a bottle of Cristal," Leland offered warmly.

"My wife will like that," Antonio said, approving. "Oh, and there is one more thing."

Leland's fingers tightened on the phone, but he kept a smile in his voice. "What's that?"

"I've decided to pay you the balance in cash. I have found myself with some…additional inventory."

Cash? Leland raised a brow. The risk factor and chance of error with banks, though small, still existed, but cash would guarantee payment immediately. And what the hell, who couldn't use a suitcase full of greenbacks lying around?

"Whatever makes it easy for you, Antonio." Smiling, Leland leaned back in his desk chair. "Three o'clock tomorrow, then."

Leland hung up the phone, then punched in Edmunds' number for the second time that day and pushed Send. It wasn't unusual that the man didn't answer his phone. Often there were long hours when he couldn't be reached, especially when he was working.

Hopefully, that annoying Blake woman and Blackhawk had been dealt with by now, but whether they had or hadn't didn't really matter at this point. Even if they showed up in Corpus Christi, they'd be chasing their own tails for days.

Leland glanced at his wristwatch. It was already five-thirty in the afternoon. In less than twenty-four hours, the babies would be delivered, Teresa Bellochio would be paid off and Leland Worthington would be long gone.

Chapter 14

At seven o'clock that evening, Rebecca waited in the truck with Bowie while Dillon checked them into a motel on the beach. After hours of staring at nothing but mesquite and flat, hard dirt, the coastline on the Gulf of Mexico was a welcome relief.

Puffy white clouds dotted the clear sky, and the ocean, a deep blue, disappeared into the horizon. Colorful sailboats glided across the water and farther out, a flock of seagulls circled a fishing boat. Postcard perfect, she thought.

Except for the fact that somewhere in this city there was a man who wanted both her and Dillon dead.

There was no proof yet that Leon Waters was in Corpus Christi. But Rebecca didn't need any proof. He was here. She couldn't explain it, but she could *feel* it. She glanced at the city buildings that rose up along the coastline and stretched as far as the eye could see.

We're going to find you, you bastard.

From the moment Rebecca had made her decision to find Waters, she'd felt a sense of urgency. An urgency that seemed to grow as each day passed. And now that they were so close, that urgency became oppressive.

"You okay?"

She jumped at the sound of Dillon's voice, hadn't even heard him open the truck door. "Fine," she said with a nod, though her pulse had quickened.

Dillon grabbed their bags and Rebecca followed him across the parking lot while Bowie, thrilled to finally be out of the truck, raced around them, barking with excitement.

The room had a kitchenette, living area and bedroom. Dillon dumped their bags on the floor beside the king-size bed. "We should get something to eat."

She hadn't even thought about food since the incident with the big rig. Her insides had been too wound up, her nerves stretched too tight. "All right."

"The pier is not far from here," he said. "A walk would probably do us some good."

Her legs felt watery, she realized, but she nodded. "Okay."

She started to turn, but suddenly his hand snaked out and grabbed her, then yanked her against him. His mouth dropped down on hers, hard and demanding. She kissed him back, slid her hands up his strong shoulders, then wrapped her arms tightly around his neck.

More than food, this was what she needed, what he needed. His kiss gentled, deepened, and she thought her bones might melt from the heat pulsing through her veins. His large hands cupped her bottom and lifted her body intimately with his. His arousal pressed into the V of her aching thighs. She moved her hips against him, felt the low moan rumble up from deep in his throat. "I want to be inside you," he murmured, trailing kisses down her neck.

His words excited her, empowered her, and now it was she who took charge. She laid her palms on his chest and pushed away from him, then reached for the bedroom door and closed it. Shutting them off from the outside world

She lifted her gaze to his, then reached for the snap on her jeans and opened it. A muscle jumped in his jaw when she slowly pulled the zipper down.

She moved toward him.

His eyes glinted black when she began to unbutton her blouse. When she stood in front of him, she slid the garment off her shoulders. It fell to the floor with a cottony whisper.

His breathing had deepened, his mouth hardened. Her simple white cotton bra had not been designed to heat a man's blood, but the way Dillon was looking at her, as if she were an ice-cream cone on a hot day, made her feel like a goddess. She slid one bra strap down her arm, then the other, then reached behind her back and unclasped the hook. The bra joined her blouse on the floor.

"So pretty." He reached out and covered her small breasts with his hands, then dropped to his knees. "So sweet."

With the pads of his rough thumbs, he circled her nipples, then pressed his mouth to her bare stomach. Rebecca let her head drop back, felt each and every exquisite sensation of his thumbs and his lips. She laid her hands on his shoulders, felt the ripple of hard muscles under her fingertips.

And then his lips replaced his hands, drew her swollen flesh into his mouth. His hot, wet tongue slid over her beaded nipple, his teeth nipped, then lightly bit. She sucked in a breath at the lightning bolt of pleasure that shot through her, then moaned.

His hands slid down her narrow waist, over her flat stomach, then inched denim and underwear slowly down her hips, her legs, until she was naked. Fire raced over her skin. She dug her fingers into his shoulders, trembled with the need pulsing through her.

His mouth moved down her belly again and his hands caressed her breasts. Certain she could stand no more, she covered his hands with her own, intending to push them away, but moving with him instead. His callused palms on her smooth, swollen flesh, her hands on his, aroused her beyond anything she'd ever experienced. Gasping, she broke the contact, then stepped back toward the bed.

Holding her gaze steady with his, she yanked the bed cover off, then lay on the cool sheets.

"Now," she whispered.

She ran her hands down her neck, her breasts, her stomach, then stroked her fingertips across the juncture of her thighs and slightly parted her legs.

His eyes narrowed darkly as he feasted his gaze on her. A sheen of sweat dampened his bronze, muscled body. His long hair fell wildly over his broad shoulders. He unsnapped his jeans, then pulled the zipper down.

Erotic. Primitive. Pagan. This was all those things, Rebecca thought, watching him shove his jeans down. He was fully aroused, hard and ready and beautifully naked.

She shivered in anticipation.

His gaze never left hers as he lowered himself onto the bed. As she had done, he slid his hands down her neck, her breasts, her stomach, then traced the soft dark curls between her legs with his fingertips.

Her heart pounded fiercely, her chest rose and fell, shallow, gasping breaths. She arched her hips upward against his hand, wanting him inside her, but he ignored her, torturing her with soft, gentle caresses between her thighs.

The sheets fisted in her hands. She closed her eyes, then she bit her lower lip to keep from crying out. God, couldn't he see how much she needed him?

His hands slowly slid up her legs, then tightened suddenly just above her knees. "Look at me," he growled.

She opened her eyes, met his black gaze. He owned her, she realized. Body and soul. But she knew in her heart that she owned part of him, as well. She lifted her arms over her head and curved her lips into a smile.

His body stiffened, then he spread her legs and surged deeply inside her.

She wrapped herself around him, held on tightly, moved with him. They were both frantic now, both clutching at each other, gasping for breath, moaning. His thrusts grew harder, deeper, and when her release came, she cried out, arching upward as the rippling pleasure washed over her again and again. Tossing his head back, Dillon groaned, his body convulsing with his climax.

Neither one of them could move. He lay heavily on top of her, but she didn't mind. She pressed her lips to his damp forehead, found the strength to slide her hand over his shoulder and smile.

It seemed as if she'd known him forever. As if she'd loved him forever. The thought of being without him when this was over was too painful to consider. So she didn't. She simply held him, felt the wonderful weight of his body on hers, the slide of his skin, the touch of his mouth on her shoulder. At this moment, it was all that mattered.

When they could ignore their empty stomachs no longer, they showered, then walked down the beach and ate shrimp and fries on the pier, drank beer and listened to a live jazz band.

He kept his cell phone with him, and they were both aware of it in the front pocket of his jeans. Both waiting for the phone call.

It came the next morning, waking them just after eight-thirty. Dillon sat on the edge of the bed, scribbling on a bedside notepad while he listened. When he hung up, he dragged a hand through his hair, then turned and looked at Rebecca.

"Well?" she asked anxiously when he didn't say anything.

One corner of his mouth curved up. "Got him."

Teresa heard a baby cry.

At first, the sound was so far away, so soft, that she thought she'd imagined it. Probably a television, she told herself, or maybe a kitten. But then she heard it again. A little louder, a little stronger.

She sat, listened carefully. Nothing.

Since she'd stopped taking the pills the doctor and Elena gave her every few hours, the fog had lifted from her mind. She was able to think more clearly and her arms and legs didn't feel so heavy. Even the man in the corner had disappeared.

Now she was hearing things.

Teresa pushed aside the breakfast tray Elena had brought a little while ago. She hadn't been hungry, but she'd forced herself to eat a few bites of scrambled eggs and some toast, knew that if she wanted to leave here, she needed her strength. She glanced at the envelope sitting beside the breakfast tray. Inside was a check for five thousand dollars and a plane ticket for Los Angeles. Teresa had tried to give the money and ticket back. They'd already done so much for her, and certainly there was someone who needed it more than she did.

But Dr. Wilson had insisted. He'd told her a

new life far away from Texas would help heal her pain. She didn't believe that, but he'd been so nice, she couldn't bring herself to argue.

With a sigh, she lowered her head to her pillow, then frowned. There it was again. Coming from an outer room. A baby's cry. The sound made her breasts feel heavy and her nipples ache.

Tossing the bed covers off, she eased herself over the side of the bed, then slid her bare feet to the tiled floor. It was the first time she'd stood by herself and it took a moment for the room to stop spinning. She knew she shouldn't go, knew that seeing another woman's baby would only deepen her pain, but she couldn't stop herself. She *had* to go.

Slowly, carefully, she made her way to the door and turned the knob, then stepped into the hallway. She heard the murmur of voices from a room at the end of the hall, Dr. Wilson and Elena, she thought, and the soft mewling of a baby. Just one quick look, she told herself, then she'd go back to her room.

With her hand on her wall to steady herself, Teresa quietly made her way down the hall, then peeked around the corner into a cozy living room with a beige sofa and blue braided rug. The doctor and Elena stood in a dining room at the opposite side of the room, their backs to her. Elena was packing diapers and bottles into a bag and the doctor was on the phone.

Teresa heard the baby's cry again, realized it came from a bassinet beside the sofa. She moved closer, then glanced inside.

Not one baby, but two, she realized. One wrapped in pink, the other in blue. So tiny, so precious. She gripped the front of her gown, felt the fresh slice of pain in her heart. Only the round curve of a cheek and a button nose was visible on the baby in pink. The baby in blue had his eyes open. They were deep blue, his shiny tuft of hair soft black. He stopped crying when she bent over him. His sweet face melted her insides.

Desperately she wanted to hold the baby, but she knew she couldn't, so she simply reached down and touched his tiny fist. She'd never felt skin so soft. She smoothed her hand over the edge of his blanket, and her fingertips brushed against a small slip of paper tucked inside and it fell out. She picked it up, intending to put it back, but when she saw the words written there, her heart stopped.

Bellochio. Boy. Five pounds, four oz.

What? She stared at the slip of paper, read it a second, then third time.

Her heart raced now, her hand shook as she pulled a second slip of paper from the little girl.

Bellochio. Girl. Five pounds, three oz.

"Oh my God!"

Elena's shout startled Teresa. She dropped the

piece of paper, watched as the nurse rushed at her, then grabbed her arm.

"Dammit, I told you to keep that door locked," Dr. Wilson yelled at Elena.

Elena's grip tightened on Teresa's arm and she yelled back at the doctor. "You *idiot*. You came out of there last."

"I—I don't understand." Teresa watched the doctor fumble in a leather satchel sitting on the table, then she looked at Elena. "Are these my babies?"

"Of course not." Elena gently pulled on Teresa's arm. "Come back to bed, honey. Don't do this to yourself."

"I'm not doing anything." Teresa yanked her arm away, was surprised at the strength surging through her. "Something's wrong here."

"Teresa—"

"These are my babies, aren't they?" Teresa grabbed the nurse and shook her. The woman's face turned white. *"Tell me!"*

"You're hallucinating," Elena said. "You didn't have twins, remember?"

Confused, Teresa tightened her grip on the nurse. She didn't remember, couldn't remember, anything.

And then suddenly the doctor wrapped his arms around her from behind and pressed a cloth over her nose. The fumes burned her lungs and blurred her eyes. She struggled against him, tried to shove him away, but he was too strong.

She heard the baby's soft cry again. The room slowly faded, then turned to black.

Leland dressed casual. Armani navy blazer, tan slacks, white polo shirt and deck shoes. He stared at his image in the full-length bathroom mirror. *You are one good-looking son of a bitch*, he thought, smoothing a hand over the side of his hair.

He'd look magnificent at the helm of his yacht. The warm sun on his face, the glorious scent of the open sea. Nothing but blue ocean and sky. He'd slaved his entire life to come to this moment and at last the day was here. Excitement rushed through him, made his pulse quicken and his breathing deepen. God, he couldn't wait.

He'd called his secretary ten minutes ago and asked her to cancel his appointments. A family emergency, he'd explained. Later today, paychecks would be delivered by a private dispatch company, along with a note explaining that the office was now officially closed and their services were no longer necessary. By that time, he'd be long gone.

"Mr. Worthington, sir, your breakfast is ready."

"Dammit, Sidwell." Startled, Leland turned

sharply at the sound of his butler's voice. The man stood at the bathroom door. "Must you always sneak around like that?"

"I'm sorry, sir." The butler's deep-set eyes shifted to the suitcase sitting beside the open closet door. "Are you going somewhere, sir?"

"My mother has taken a turn for the worse and I'm flying to Ohio to be with her." Leland had mentioned his "sick mother" to enough people, that no one would question his sudden departure. "I'll be gone for an indefinite period of time."

"I'm terribly sorry," the butler said. "Is there anything I can do?"

"Actually, Sidwell, I'm afraid I have to let you go." Leland reached into the pocket of his blazer and pulled out an envelope. "I've written a letter of recommendation and given you a severance check."

Confused, the butler stared at the envelope. "I— I don't understand, sir."

"I'm sure you'll find employment elsewhere," Leland said. "I'd like you to be gone within the hour."

"Within the hour?" Sidwell repeated, his usual dull tone edged with disbelief.

"Sooner, if possible." When Leland's cell phone rang, he pressed the envelope into the butler's hand. "That will be all."

"Yes, sir." Sidwell stared at the envelope, then backed away. "Thank you, sir."

Leland waited a moment for the butler to leave the room, then flipped open his phone. "Worthington."

"Leland," Antonio said cheerfully. "We've just checked into our hotel and the wife is suddenly anxious to complete our business. Can you be at the Marriott in an hour? Suite 732."

"The Marriott in an hour?" Leland glanced at his watch. It was only nine-thirty. Damn if Medini didn't keep him hopping. But the sooner they made the exchange, the better. Not hearing from Edmunds since yesterday had made him uneasy. "Sure, no problem."

Leland had barely ended the call when his phone rang again.

"Yes?"

"We've got a problem," the doctor said at the other end of the line.

"I'm sorry, Miss Roberts, but Mr. Worthington isn't in the office at the moment." The secretary's tone was businesslike and terse. "May I take a message?"

Rebecca glanced at Dillon, who had his ear to the cell phone. They were parked on the street outside Leon Waters'—aka Leland Worthington's— office building. Dillon gestured for Rebecca to keep talking.

"Will he be back in today?" Rebecca asked.

"It's really very important that I speak with him personally."

"What's this regarding?" the secretary asked.

"My—my husband, Thurston—" Rebecca made her voice quiver. "He passed away unexpectedly last week, and five million dollars is simply so overwhelming."

Dillon mouthed the word "Thurston" and lifted a brow. Rebecca ignored him.

"I'm so sorry for your loss." Sympathy softened the secretary's voice. "My name is Rita. I'm Mr. Worthington's personal assistant. Perhaps I can schedule an appointment for you next week?"

"If I could just speak with Mr. Worthington, even for a minute—" Rebecca broke off with a sob. "Forgive me, Rita. Except for little Thurston, I'm all alone now. I don't know who I can trust."

"Well, you can certainly trust us," the secretary reassured Rebecca. "I'll tell you what. I'll try to contact Mr. Worthington at his residence and if you give me a number, I'll call you right back."

Rebecca looked at Dillon, but he shook his head.

"If it's all right—" Rebecca made her voice waver "—I'll call you after the service this morning."

"Of course it's all right, dear," Rita said. "I'll wait for your call."

Rebecca hung up and handed the phone to Dillon. "So he's not at the office."

"Which leaves his apartment." Dillon started the truck engine and pulled into traffic. "We're about ten minutes away."

Dillon's contact had provided not only Leon Waters' alias of Leland Worthington, but his business and home address, as well.

"What if he's not there?" she asked, worrying her bottom lip. "What then?"

"One step at a time, sweetheart." Dillon turned right at the next corner, then handed Rebecca the map he'd stuck under his leg. "You navigate."

Wednesday morning traffic was light and eight minutes later, Dillon parked across the street from the Shoredrive Luxury Apartments. Rebecca reached to unbuckle her seat belt and Dillon put a hand on her arm. "I can do this easier by myself."

"Not a chance, Blackhawk." Rebecca shook her head. Dillon had already tried to make her stay behind with Bowie at the motel, but she'd refused. "I didn't come this far to sit in the car by myself."

He stared at her for a long moment and she could see he wanted to argue, but he blew out a breath and let go of her arm instead. "You do exactly what I say, when I say. Got it?"

She nodded, then felt her heart skip when Dillon pulled his gun out of the console and shoved it under his black T-shirt. The last time he'd done that, she remembered, someone had turned up dead.

The Shoredrive Luxury Apartments had a view of a busy marina and the Bay Front in downtown Corpus Christi. Somewhere in the distance, a ship's foghorn sounded and a buoy clanged. An ocean breeze cooled the air and ruffled the fronds on the palm trees lining the street.

"Apartment 2204," Dillon said.

"What about security?" Rebecca asked when they crossed the street.

"There's a camera over the entrance." Dillon casually looped an arm around Rebecca's shoulders. "Just keep your head down."

Her pulse raced when they walked under the camera, then through the tall glass entry doors. The lobby was elegant, with black marbled floors, burgundy leather sofas and plush damask print chairs. Two elderly women standing by a potted fern paused in their conversation when Dillon pressed the elevator button. He glanced over his shoulder and smiled at the women.

"Morning, ladies. You're looking lovely today."

The women both blushed, then quickly looked away.

The elevator *pinged* and the doors opened.

"Aren't you the charmer?" Rebecca spared him a glance as he punched the elevator button.

When the elevator stopped, Dillon pulled his gun out from under his T-shirt. "Stay behind me."

Adrenaline pumped through her veins as they walked down the hall. Number 2204 was at the very end.

Dillon motioned for Rebecca to move against the wall, then stood to the side of the door and knocked.

He waited, then knocked a second time. A man opened the door and stuck his head out.

Dillon put his gun to the man's temple.

Chapter 15

Leland drove to the suburbs and parked his silver Mercedes in front of the small white clapboard house at 966 Tustin Avenue. Technically, he owned the place, though he'd never actually been here. The house was one of three he'd bought through the Ray of Light Foundation, a nonprofit organization that he'd established after he'd moved to Corpus Christi, but no matter how deep anyone dug, they'd never find the name Leland Worthington on any document. He had a magic touch when it came to moving money around from ledger to ledger, from account to account, until *poof!*—it suddenly disappeared. The system had been perfect.

He'd been unstoppable.

I still am.

Leland shut off his engine and stared at the house. Normally he would never handle such a mundane problem like this himself. But with Antonio waiting for him, time was critical. He glanced at his watch. Nine fifty-eight. Even with this minor setback, he would make it to the Marriot by ten-thirty.

He didn't hurry, knew that any busybody neighbor who might be watching would simply see a well-dressed man calmly strolling up the walk to the house. Even if they remembered his car, it didn't matter. After today, Leland Worthington would no longer exist.

When he raised his hand to knock on the door, it flew open. A wide-eyed brunette stood there, clutching nervously at the front of her green print sundress. He'd never met the woman, but he knew it was Wilson's girlfriend, Elena. "Mr. Worthington, thank you so much for—"

He pushed past her and moved into the living room, saw the doctor sitting on the sofa, holding his head in his hands. Leland walked directly to the man, grabbed him by the collar and yanked him to his feet. "You *moron*."

"I can explain—"

Leland slammed his fist into Wilson's cheek. With a grunt, the doctor stumbled to the floor.

"Bobby!" Elena rushed to the doctor's side and knelt, then glared at Leland. "What did you do that for? He didn't do—"

Because he still needed the woman and didn't want to leave a mark on her face, Leland slapped his palm hard against the side of Elena's head. She cried out and crumpled on the floor next to the doctor.

"You're both incompetent," Leland sneered. "Bobby boy here is a cokehead who wouldn't even have a license to practice if it weren't for me, and you were working strip joints until he picked you up a year ago. Now get up and tell me what happened."

Holding on to each other, the doctor and Elena stood, dazed and crouching in fear.

"She came out here." The doctor dragged a shaking hand through his hair. "She saw the babies, knew they were hers."

"You were supposed to keep her drugged," Leland said tightly.

"We did," Elena shot back, her courage returning. "We stood over her while she took the pills, watched her swallow them. An elephant would be drowsy with the dosage we were giving her."

Leland glanced around the living room. "Where's the mother?"

"Locked in the bedroom," Wilson said. "Out cold. I used chloroform on her."

"And the babies?"

"At the other end of the house where we usually keep them," the woman said. "In a bedroom off the kitchen."

Leland looked at Elena. "Get them in your car."

"But we can't go through with this now," Wilson insisted. "We just want our money, not all of it, maybe just half. Enough so we can start a new life somewhere."

"You don't get it, do you?" Leland grabbed the doctor's shirt and shook him. "We either deliver these babies or we don't have a life. A deal with Antonio Medini is like making a deal with the devil himself. If we don't deliver, we all go straight to hell."

"But the mother knows," Elena complained. "She can identify us."

Leland wondered how two people so stupid had ever made it to adulthood. "She's distraught. We're going to give her something to calm her down. Permanently."

Elena gasped. "We don't want no part of that. Tell him, Bobby. We never signed on to kill nobody."

Enough of these idiots, Leland thought and pulled the gun out of his blazer jacket. He pointed it directly at the doctor's heart. "You signed on to do what I say, when I say. Now I'd rather not use this, because I really hate blood. But you've got three seconds to get your bag of tricks or I'm going to put a fucking hole through you. And you—" he turned the gun toward the woman "—get those damn babies in the car and shut your stupid trap."

Eyes bulging, Elena slowly backed away. "Okay, okay. Take it easy. Whatever you say, Mr. Worthington."

Leland brought the barrel of the gun back to the doctor, who nodded, then turned and hurried toward a leather bag sitting on a dining table.

He glanced at his watch. They still had plenty of time to take care of Teresa Bellochio and get to the Marriot. The woman's body wouldn't be found for days, and she'd just be another Jane Doe. With no family or friends looking for her, the chances of an ID any time soon were between slim and none.

Wilson came back holding two vials of clear liquid and a syringe. His hands were shaking.

"That's better," Leland said, smiling. "Now let's do it."

Wake up…wake up…

Teresa heard the voice whispering in her ear, felt the rush of cool air over her face. She heard the sound of a moan, realized it came from her own throat.

Wake up…hurry…

She sat, lifted a trembling hand to her temple, then blinked to clear her vision.

She was back in her room, on the bed, but she didn't remember how she'd gotten here.

And then suddenly everything rushed back at her.

Her babies. *Two* babies. She'd had twins.

They were alive.

The reality of it pumped strength into her blood, into her arms and legs. She didn't understand what was happening, but she understood she was in danger, that her babies were in danger. She let her heart guide her. Her heart and the voice whispering in her ear.

Hurry...

She slid out of bed, shoved her pillow under the covers and pulled the sheets high. They would come for her, that much she understood. She knew too much now. She glanced around the room, looking for a weapon, anything that might help her, but what did she know about weapons? Not once in her life had she hurt a living thing.

Until this moment, she wouldn't have thought she could hurt another person, even to defend herself. But now she knew she could.

Now she knew she could kill.

A rage built inside her. For her babies, for herself. Like a storm, it grew, swirled deep inside her with white-hot fury. Her fingers closed into fists, her jaw tightened. A growl rumbled low in her throat. She would do whatever she had to do.

Her gaze scanned the room, but there was nothing that could help her. She staggered to the bathroom, but again, there was nothing except a towel and a bar of soap. She opened the medicine cabinet over the sink, but it was empty. When she closed it, Teresa stared at herself in the mirror, barely recognized herself.

She glanced down at the towel, then wrapped it around her hand and smashed her fist into the mirror. Her reflection shattered. She struck the mirror again and thick shards fell into the sink. Quickly she wrapped one end of the towel around the largest piece, then stumbled back into the room.

At the sound of a key in the lock, she ducked behind the door, her pulse racing, her weapon poised.

The door opened slowly, and she heard the doctor's voice.

"Teresa," he called softly. "It's Dr. Wilson."

She saw the syringe in his hand, felt her heart slam against her ribs. *You bastard,* she wanted to scream, but she held her breath, waited.

He opened the door a little wider and stepped inside the room. "Teresa—"

She swung her arm down, sank the sharp end of the jagged glass into the doctor's neck. He shrieked in pain, then dropped to his knees. She shoved him away and bolted through the doorway.

A fist caught her on the chin and she saw stars, then stumbled backward and landed on the tiled floor. The taste of blood filled her mouth. Slowly, she lifted her head, watched as a second man wearing a navy jacket stepped into the room. He was older, his hair silver-gray.

He pointed the gun in his hand directly at her.

On a sob, Teresa closed her eyes.

"Well, Miss Bellochio." The man clucked his tongue in disapproval. "You've been quite a handful."

She tried to stand, but the room was still spinning. "Why…are you…doing this to me?"

"You did this to yourself, I'm afraid," he said. "You could have walked out of here, a nice little check in your hands and a plane ticket to anywhere you wanted."

"My babies," she whispered weakly.

"They will have everything you could possibly want for them. Money, privilege, respect. The best education. What could you have given them?"

"You don't know me," she said through clenched teeth. "You know nothing about me."

The man sighed heavily, then looked at the doctor. "Wilson! Stop your goddamn sniveling and pick up that syringe."

"She stabbed me," the doctor whined, holding his neck. Blood seeped through his fingers.

"And I'm going to shoot you if you don't pick up that syringe right now."

"Please don't do this," she pleaded. "Please."

Helpless to stop what was happening, Teresa watched the doctor pick up the syringe and move toward her.

Dillon parked the truck in front of the house next door to 966 Tustin Avenue. The neighborhood was quiet and except for a mail truck at the opposite end of the block, the street was deserted.

He'd driven like a bat out of hell from the apartment complex and they'd made good time.

"That's his car." Dillon looked at the silver Mercedes Roadster parked by the curb, then glanced at Rebecca. He wanted to tell her to wait in the car, but based on the glint of determination in her green eyes, he might as well be talking to the steering wheel.

"You stay behind me, understand?"

She nodded, then they both opened their doors at the same time and sprinted toward the house, cutting across the lawn and crouching down behind a row of bushes under the front windows. With Rebecca on his heels, Dillon leaped onto the front porch and pressed against the wall beside the door.

He held his gun at his side and reached for the doorknob, gently twisted.

It turned.

Slowly, Dillon pushed the door open and stepped inside, then quickly scanned the room. It was empty, but he heard the sound of men's voices from the hallway to the left, then a woman's soft cry. Lifting his gun, he peeked around the corner into the hallway, saw the open door. He motioned for Rebecca to watch the living room, then crept down the hall.

"For God's sake," Dillon heard a man say, "will you just do it?"

Dillon stepped behind a gray-haired man standing just inside the door. "You move, your friend moves, and you're both dead."

The gray-haired man stiffened, started to turn, but froze when Dillon cocked the trigger on his gun. "Ah-ah. Now drop your gun, nice and easy, then kick it away."

The gun dropped to the floor with a thud.

Dillon touched the barrel of his gun to the back of the man's head. "I said, *kick it away.*"

The gun skittered across the tile.

Dillon glanced at the second man who was kneeling on the floor. Blood dripped from the man's neck, staining the white doctor's coat he wore. He had the needle of a syringe pressed to a young woman's arm. "Drop that," Dillon warned. *"Now!"*

Eyes wide with terror, the doctor dropped the

syringe. The woman shoved the man away, then scrambled backward.

The gray-haired man lifted his hands and Dillon saw the light reflect off the diamond he wore on his left pinky finger.

Waters.

"It's been a long time, Leon," Dillon said in disgust. "Oh, that's right, it's Leland now."

"I have no idea what you're talking about." Leland turned slowly, his gaze locked on the gun pointed at him. "But this is none of your business."

"Is that so? What do you say, Rebecca? You think this is our business?"

Rebecca stepped beside him, her eyes narrowed as she stared at the man they knew as Leon Waters. "Radick and Edmunds send their regards," she said coldly.

Waters's head came up. "How did you find me here?"

"Never piss off your butler," Dillon said. "They always know way more than you'd ever think."

From his peripheral vision, Dillon saw the movement to his right and turned his head, saw the woman standing openmouthed in the middle of the living room. The distraction, though barely a split second, was enough for Leon to lunge forward and grab Dillon's hand.

They struggled for the gun, crashed backward

into the wall, smashing plaster. A woman screamed, then cursed shrilly. Leon twisted Dillon's hand and the gun dropped to the floor. They both scrambled for it, but it was out of their reach. Leon swung his fist into Dillon's mouth, then his stomach; Dillon countered with a blow to the other man's nose.

Howling in pain, Leon covered his nose with his hands and staggered backward, then dropped to his knees. Blood rushed down his chin and dripped to the floor. Dillon glanced toward the living room, saw that Rebecca had knocked out the woman in the living room with a brass candlestick.

Dillon rose to his feet and wiped the back of his hand across his mouth, barely noticed the blood there. He smiled at Rebecca. "Not bad," he said.

She grinned back. "Not so bad yourself."

Dillon watched the grin on Rebecca's face fade. "Dillon," she whispered, "turn around."

He turned, saw the young woman standing in the doorway, staring at Leon. She held Leon's gun in her hands, had the barrel pointed at his head.

"Where are my babies?" the woman asked with deadly calm.

"Don't." Dillon slowly lifted a hand. "Don't do it."

"They told me my baby had died." Her voice shook. "I didn't even know I had two. What kind of monster could do such a thing?"

"He'll go to jail." Dillon moved closer, kept his voice soft and soothing. "They will all go to jail. Put the gun down."

"Where are my babies?" she screamed at Leon and cocked the trigger. "Tell me!"

"I suggest you answer the woman." Dillon looked at Leon, whose tanned face had turned white.

"In the bedroom." Leon covered his arms over his head, as if he might ward off a bullet. "Off the kitchen."

"What's your name?" Dillon asked softly, stepping beside the woman.

"Teresa," she answered quietly. "Teresa Bellochio."

"Teresa." Carefully, Dillon stretched out his hand. "My name is Dillon. Dillon Blackhawk. This is Rebecca Blake. We're here now. Everything is all right."

Teresa slowly looked up, met Dillon's steady gaze. Tears streamed down her cheeks. Trembling, she handed the gun to Dillon. When Leon lowered his arms, Dillon kicked the man in the face and he fell forward, unconscious. Inside the bedroom, the man with the neck wound was writhing on the floor, crying that he needed a doctor.

"My babies," Teresa whispered, clutching at Dillon's arm.

"They're right here." Rebecca stood in the living room, holding a blue bundle in one arm, a pink bundle in the other.

On a sob, Teresa flew across the room, touched one tiny face with a fingertip, then the other.

"They're beautiful," Rebecca said, handing first one baby, then the other to their mother.

Teresa held them close, rocking them and cooing lightly, kissing their soft cheeks. "Mommy's here," she whispered. "Mommy's here."

In the distance, the sound of sirens filled the air.

Uniformed officers and detectives crawled over every inch of the house on Tustin street, inside and out. Lights flashed on the ambulance parked at the street, two-way radios crackled loudly, and a small crowd of neighbors had gathered on the lawn across the street to watch the unfolding drama.

On the sofa in the living room, Rebecca sat beside Teresa, listened in shock and amazement as the young woman related the past four days to a Detective Janet Rellas.

Rebecca hoped that all of them—Waters, Dr. Wilson and Elena—rotted in prison for the rest of their miserable lives.

The wounded doctor had been taken away on a stretcher a few minutes ago and the nurse had been handcuffed and escorted to a squad car, then driven off. Leon, or Leland, as he called himself now, was still being questioned in the back bedroom. Dillon sat at the dining room table and gave a statement to a uniformed officer.

It's over, Rebecca thought. *It's finally over.*

Rebecca looked at the two sleeping babies Teresa held in her arms. The detective had offered help, but Teresa had refused. After the story Rebecca had just heard, she doubted that Teresa would ever let anyone near her children again.

And who would blame her? Rebecca stared at the two tiny bundles and felt her heart melt.

That's what this had all been about, Rebecca realized. Why she'd felt the urgency, the driving need, to find Waters. To bring them to this moment, to help this woman and her children. It hadn't just been about what Waters had done in the past, though he would certainly have to pay for that. It was about what he'd intended to do in the *present*.

She could never tell anyone that, of course. Who would believe such craziness? She glanced up at Dillon, saw that he was watching her.

He would believe.

The bedroom door opened. Instinct had Teresa clutching her babies tighter when an officer led a handcuffed Leon into the living room. The man's nose and right eye had swollen. *It's not enough,* Rebecca thought. When the man glared at her, she lifted her chin and met his cold gaze.

Dillon rose from the dining room table and moved beside Rebecca and Teresa.

"You're just like your father," Leon said in disgust.

Dillon stiffened. "I'm nothing like my father."

Leon slowly smiled. "Yeah, you are. You just don't know it."

The officer grabbed Leon's arm. "Let's go."

"We're going to take you and your babies to the hospital to be examined now," Detective Rellas told Teresa. "Is there anyone you'd like us to call? Any family or friends you'd like to have with you?"

"There's no one," Teresa said, shaking her head, then looked from Rebecca to Dillon. "Would you…could you—"

Rebecca opened her mouth to answer, but it was Dillon who spoke the words she'd been about to say.

"Of course we will."

Chapter 16

Rebecca quietly closed the bedroom door behind her and stepped into the living area of the motel suite. Bowie greeted her with an enthusiastic lick on her hand, then the animal resumed the watch he'd taken up outside the bedroom door.

Like his master, Bowie had been fiercely protective of Teresa and her babies, as if the dog somehow knew what the young woman had been through and he now considered it his sole duty to protect them.

"They're asleep," she said softly when Dillon turned from the open patio sliding door.

"Good."

Rebecca lifted a hand to smooth back her hair, then stopped midair. Brown grocery store bags covered the dining table and department shopping bags covered the sofa. Two bassinets filled with baby items stood side by side in the entryway.

"What's all this?"

"I figured Teresa would need a few things," he said with a shrug. "I made a couple of phone calls."

A couple of phone calls? Rebecca looked at all the bags and baby paraphernalia. Heavens, she'd only been in the bedroom helping Teresa shower and feed her babies for a little more than an hour. How in the world did the man manage to make things happen so quickly?

It was as if life were on fast forward these past few days, she realized. From the first night she'd walked into the Backwater Saloon, everything had happened at warp speed.

Would it end just as quickly? she wondered, then put the thought from her mind. She didn't want to think about that right now.

The scent of the ocean drifted in through the open patio slider, and a breeze gently lifted the corner of the drapes. For the first time in days, perhaps in months, Rebecca felt a sense of peace.

Folding her arms, she moved toward Dillon and looked up at him. "Dillon Blackhawk, you're a big phony."

He lifted a brow. "Is that so?"

"Yeah, that's so. You want everyone to think you're big and tough and mean."

"I *am* big and tough and mean." He scowled at her to prove it.

She shook her head, then placed her palms flat on his wide, hard chest, felt the steady beat of his heart. "You're really just a marshmallow inside."

His scowl deepened. "If you were a man, you know I'd have to beat you up for saying that."

Smiling, she slid her hands up his shoulders and around his neck, then pulled his head down to hers. "Aren't I glad I'm not a man."

His lips touched hers gently at first, then his strong arms came around her and his mouth claimed hers. His kiss was long and deep, consuming, and she reveled in the pleasure rippling through her.

With a sigh, she pulled away, then laid her head on his chest and looked out at the ocean waves crashing on the beach. "He almost killed her."

"He didn't."

"When she had the gun on him." Rebecca lifted her head and looked into Dillon's eyes. "Part of me wanted her to pull the trigger. But then I realized that there are other babies out there, other people he's hurt, and I knew he had to live."

"Where he's going, he'll never hurt anyone

again," Dillon said. "Between Dr. Wilson's and Elena's confessions and the butler's cooperation, the police already have enough to put him away for ten lifetimes."

"It's not enough," Rebecca said firmly. But at least the police would have a place to start, she thought.

"Don't think about him anymore." Dillon tucked a loose strand of hair behind Rebecca's ear. "Tell me about the babies."

"They're so beautiful." She smiled, knew that Dillon was diverting her, but she didn't mind. "Cade sucks his formula down like there's no tomorrow, and he gets cranky when you burp him, but Carissa is as delicate and dainty as a little flower."

"Did Teresa tell you anything about herself?"

Rebecca shook her head. "I didn't ask. I figured if and when she wants to talk, she knows she can trust me. The only thing I do know is that she wants no part of her family or the father. She's also made it clear she's not looking for handouts."

"There's a difference between a handout and a helping hand," Dillon said evenly.

"That's exactly what I told her." Rebecca glanced at all the shopping bags and grinned. "You're going to have to explain all this, though. She's a very determined young woman."

"Sounds like someone else I know," he said, then slid his hands down her arms and sighed. "Rebecca…"

Her heart sank when his voice trailed off and he shifted awkwardly. *Not yet,* she wanted to say. *Please not yet. Just let us have one more day, one more hour, even, before you walk out of my life.*

She'd known this moment would come, but she wasn't ready. *As if she'd ever be ready to watch the man she loved walk out of her life.*

She wouldn't cry, dammit. Not now, anyway. There'd be plenty of time for tears later. Lifting her chin, she looked at him and waited. If he had something to say, he better just say it.

"I'm leaving tomorrow."

Tomorrow? A knife in her heart couldn't have cut as sharp or hurt as deep. Still, she held her chin high, wondered why his hand was suddenly trembling when he was the one leaving. She said nothing, was damned if she'd make it easy for him.

"I want you to, will you…God." He stepped back, dragged a hand through his hair and looked at the ceiling. "Dammit."

This was how he would end it? she thought angrily. After everything they'd been through, he couldn't even look at her when he said goodbye?

Furious, she squared her shoulders, then poked

a finger at his chest. *"Dammit?"* she repeated the swear word and poked him again so hard he stumbled back. "That's the best you can come up with? No, 'It's been great, you were great, see you around?' Just *dammit?*"

"What are you—"

She poked him again. "If you've got something to say, Blackhawk, then just say it and stop pussyfooting around."

"I don't pussyfoot, dammit." He grabbed her hand when she moved to stab her finger at him again. "Will you come with me?"

She froze. "Come with you?"

"I'm going to Wolf River tomorrow." He squeezed her hand. "I want you to come with me."

She blinked slowly. "You're going to Wolf River?" He nodded.

"You want me to go with you?" She felt like an idiot repeating everything he said, but her brain had suddenly shut down.

"I think you should." He lifted her hand to his mouth and nibbled on her knuckles. "Neither one of us have been there in a long time. We should check it out, see if the house suits us."

"Us?" she whispered, was afraid to let herself hope.

"Well, we have to live somewhere, and while I'm willing to consider other options, I thought we should start with the Circle B."

She laid her free hand on his chest to steady herself, was afraid she might slide to the floor if she didn't. "You're pussyfooting again, Blackhawk," Rebecca said breathlessly. "For God's sake, will you just say it?"

He frowned at her, then sighed heavily. "In my heart, I think I'd always known you would come to me. But my heart was the one thing I never let myself trust, so I ran from it. Denied my past and wandered aimlessly, existing, but not living. And then you walked into my life."

"More like barged," she reminded him.

Smiling, he pulled her closer. "I couldn't run anymore, couldn't deny my past any more than I can deny my future." He cupped her cheek in his hand. "My past, my present and my future are all you, Rebecca. Only you. I love you."

Joy swelled in her chest and tears burned her eyes. He'd taken her from despair to disbelief to desperately happy in less than two minutes. She had the crazy, wonderful feeling that's how their lives together would be.

"I love you, too," she managed to say through the happiness choking her throat.

"Come with me to Wolf River." He pressed his lips to hers. "Meet my family. Marry me. Make a life with me and our children."

Marriage. Children. Love overflowed, and she

swam in the dizzy wonder of its beauty. "Yes," she murmured and slid her arms around his neck. *"Yes."*

She'd never forget this moment. The sound of the waves crashing on the beach, the scent of the ocean, the drum of her heart against Dillon's. The touch of his mouth on hers.

Rebecca suddenly remembered the young woman sleeping in the bedroom with her babies.

"Teresa," she said, looking up into Dillon's eyes. "I can't leave her yet. It's too soon."

"Not to worry." Dillon smiled. "She's coming with us."

Rebecca raised a brow. "Does she know that?"

"She will when the reinforcements get here."

"Reinforcements?" Rebecca frowned. "What reinforce—"

A knock sounded on the door. Bowie jumped up from his guard and ran to the door, sniffing and whining. His hand tightly holding hers, Dillon dragged Rebecca across the room with him and opened the door.

"Ola, mijo! Look at you, such a sight!"

Maria!

Suitcase in her hand, with Juan right behind her, the woman burst through the door and patted Dillon's cheek, then hugged the breath out of Rebecca.

"A limousine he sends for us," Maria looked at

Rebecca and huffed. "Can you believe such a thing? As if he were a rich man!"

Rebecca looked at Dillon, who shrugged. Apparently, he needed to have a talk with Maria, but at the moment, she was too excited to listen to anything but the sound of her own voice.

"Where is our *mamacita*?" Maria said.

"Sleeping right now," Dillon said, closing the door and ruffling a grinning Juan's head.

"*Bien.*" Maria nodded, then clucked her tongue when she glanced around the room. "*Ay, caramba.* We have much to do. Hurry, Juan. Put some water on for the rice. Tonight we will cook *arroz con pollo.*"

Maria blew past them and Rebecca stared at Dillon in disbelief. "When…how?"

"Earlier today," he said with a shrug. "When you were in the hospital room with Teresa."

Shaking her head, she watched Maria dive into the grocery bags, then looked back at Dillon in disbelief. "Anything else I need to know?"

Smiling, he reached for her and pulled her into his arms. "Did I mention I love you?"

"Yeah," she whispered and leaned into him. "But I wouldn't mind hearing it again."

"I love you," he murmured and lowered his mouth to hers.

Behind them, Rebecca heard Maria sigh and

Juan giggle. She thought of Teresa sleeping in the bedroom, her sweet babies lying on the bed beside her.

Laughing, she kissed Dillon back and knew that she, that they, were all exactly where they belonged.

"This is your house?" Juan said three days later when Dillon pulled into the curved graveled driveway of the home he'd been raised in. "It is a *mansion*!"

"Not a mansion." Dillon parked in front of the large brick house and cut the truck's engine. "But it is big, isn't it? There are horses in the corral if you'd like to go see."

With a *whoop,* Juan jumped out of the front seat and Bowie was right behind him. Dog and boy tore around the side of the house. Dillon stepped out of the truck and stared at the house he'd left sixteen years ago.

He hadn't been certain what he would feel when he returned here. If the pain and anger of the past might somehow taint the happiness of the present. But the spirit of his grandfather and his mother spread light over the darkness, and Dillon knew the legacy of their love would live on through him.

He scanned the landscape that surrounded him, mile after mile of low rolling hills and large oaks. The scent of cattle and horse drifted on the hot morning air and his palms itched to ride the land again. Since William Blackhawk's death, a skeleton crew had been kept on to maintain the land and house. They'd obviously done a good job, Dillon thought, noticing the fresh coat of white paint on the house trim and the new varnish on the double oak entry doors. Even the flower beds had been recently planted and an explosion of yellow and white daisies spilled over a brick edging.

At the sound of tires crunching on gravel, Dillon turned and with a mixture of excitement and nerves, watched the black limousine pull up behind his truck. They'd all caravaned here from Corpus Christi and it had taken two days longer then he'd expected for them to arrive.

Babies had their own schedule, he'd learned over the past three days.

The limousine driver got out and nodded at Dillon, then moved around and opened the car door. Maria came out first holding little Cade, then Rebecca stepped out with Carissa in her arms. Teresa followed, arguing that she wasn't an invalid and Rebecca reluctantly handed the baby girl over to her mother. Dillon smiled, was certain that if Teresa had refused to come with them, they'd all still be in Corpus Christi until she changed her mind. Fortunately, Teresa had been overwhelmed and outnumbered.

"We are *familia* now," Maria had said, hugging the young woman. Teresa had burst into tears, then Rebecca, and then all the women were crying and hugging each other. Dillon had quietly left the motel room before they turned the waterworks on him.

Eyes wide, Maria stared at the house, then spoke under her breath quickly in Spanish and crossed herself. She was still trying to understand why a man who had so much *dinero* had been living in her garage for six months.

One of the tall, oak entry doors opened and a man in a conservative charcoal suit and blue tie stepped onto the front porch. Dillon walked up the steps and held out his hand. "Peter. Thank you for coming."

"My pleasure, sir." The executor smiled and took the hand Dillon offered. "I hope everything will meet with your satisfaction."

"We'll let the women decide that." Dillon watched the trio of females come up the steps. "I'm just a hired hand here."

"Ladies," Peter said with a bow. "Welcome to the Circle B."

While the limo driver unloaded bags and suitcases, Peter escorted Maria and Teresa to their rooms. Dillon grabbed Rebecca before she could get away and pulled her into a hallway.

"I missed you," he said, pressing her against

the wall and kissing her deeply. She slid into his kiss, was breathless by the time he finally lifted his head.

"It's only been two hours," she whispered, wrapping her arms around his neck.

"It felt like two weeks."

Smiling, she touched her lips to his, then glanced back around the corner. The marbled entry floor gleamed white and a round walnut table beside the stairway held a huge vase of fresh flowers. The scent of roses and daylilies mixed with lemon wax and floor polish.

"I used to help my mother polish the wood on the stairs," she said, then looked back at Dillon. "I slid down them once, when no one was around."

"I did that myself a time or two," he said, grinning.

Rebecca ran a fingertip down Dillon's chest. "Do you think our kids will, too?"

His hand covered hers, then he lifted her chin and looked into her eyes. "Does that mean you want to be a rancher's wife?"

"I want to be your wife, Dillon," she said, nodding. "Wherever that takes me. Wolf River, Resolute. Timbuctoo. It doesn't matter to me as long as I'm with you. My sister and brother aren't crazy about me leaving Boston, but Sean has a plane. They can visit whenever they want."

"I'll build an airstrip." He brushed his mouth

over hers. "Just don't make me wait too long, sweetheart. I've already waited a lifetime for you."

"I'll bet it's pretty here in the fall," she said softly. "An autumn wedding would be nice."

"Autumn it is." Upstairs, he heard Maria telling Teresa that she needed to rest while her babies slept. "When Maria finds out we've set a date, there'll be no stopping her."

"I know." Rebecca's eyes sparkled green. "Isn't she wonderful?"

"Yeah, I guess she is," he agreed, stole another long, mind-bending kiss, and didn't think he could wait until autumn.

He also didn't think he could wait until he got her alone and showed her how much he loved her. To say the least, the past three days had been sheer chaos, even though a good type of chaos. Watching Rebecca hold Teresa's babies and croon over them had made him anxious for children of their own. The thought of it brought a hitch to his chest, had him tightening his hold on his future bride and pulling her closer.

At the sound of a throat clearing, Dillon lifted his head, saw the man standing in the doorway. He wore jeans and a chambray shirt. To his left stood another man, also in jeans, but his shirt was white. A woman in black slacks and a blue blouse stood to the right.

Without question, all three carried the Blackhawk genes. The same dark hair, high cheekbones, dark skin.

Dillon had been expecting them, but now that they were here, his palms suddenly felt damp and his throat turned to dust. Straightening, he stepped away from Rebecca and walked to the man in front. "Rand?"

Rand nodded. Dillon looked at the second man. "Seth?"

Seth nodded, as well, then Dillon looked at the woman. "Elizabeth."

A smile touched her deep blue eyes. "My name is Clair now, but these lugs call me Lizzie sometimes."

"This is Rebecca." Dillon turned to Rebecca and reached for her.

He saw the trepidation in her green eyes as she stared at the Blackhawk siblings, then looked back at him. "Your cousins," she whispered.

Dillon slipped an arm around Rebecca's waist and tugged her against him. Having her next to him made this moment right, he realized. Made it complete.

"No," Dillon said, holding Rand's gaze. "My brothers and my sister."

"Your brothers and sister?" Rebecca repeated, then shook her head. "I—I don't understand."

Dillon raked a hand over his head and sighed, knew it wasn't going to be easy to explain. He'd had three days, and he still wasn't certain he understood it himself.

"My mother was pregnant with me when she married my—when she married William," he began, struggled to find the right words. "William knew that I was his brother Jonathan's child, that my mother loved Jonathan and not him, but he didn't care. Marrying my mother and raising me was his own sick way of revenge."

"Revenge for what?" Rebecca asked.

"William had always been jealous of both his brothers," Dillon explained. "Jonathan and Thomas had been smarter and stronger, and in William's twisted mind, he thought my grandfather favored them."

"But if Jonathan was your father, why didn't he claim you? Why didn't he—" Rebecca stopped, then looked at Rand and bit her lip. "I'm sorry, that's none of my business."

"You have nothing to be sorry for," Clair said softly, stepping forward. "If it wasn't for you and your mother's journal, none of us would be standing here now. You brought us all back together, Rebecca. For that we are eternally grateful."

Rebecca shook her head. "What my mother did was unforgivable."

Clair smiled softly. "It was as it was supposed to be. But as for your question, Jonathan didn't know that Mary carried his child. They'd only been dating a short time when he met our mother and they fell in love. Mary knew that she'd lost Jonathan, but she married William so Dillon could keep the Blackhawk name that rightfully belonged to him. She never told anyone the truth."

"But if she never told anyone—" Rebecca furrowed her brow "—then how do you know any of this?"

"Leon Waters," Dillon said dryly. "After my mother died, William got drunk and made the mistake of confiding in Leon. Leon tried to make a deal with me after he was arrested, was stupid enough to think that I might help him get a lighter sentence if he told me everything he knew. I told him to go to hell, then I called Rand."

Dillon knew that William Blackhawk's hatred had taken so much from Rand and Seth and Clair. They'd been lied to and sold off like cattle, their lives turned upside down. *How can they look at me and not see William?* Dillon thought.

It felt as if the house had suddenly drawn in a breath and held it. Dillon watched his half-brother's hand come up, then a smile slowly spread across his face.

"Welcome home, Dillon."

Dillon tightly clasped Rand's hand, felt the house breathe again. Felt himself breathe again. There were more handshakes, then hugs, then tears.

It is done, Dillon heard the quiet whisper in his ear.

"Dillon!"

He turned, watched Teresa hurrying down the stairs, hugging a wooden picture frame to her chest. Her eyes were wide, her cheeks flushed with excitement. She hesitated halfway down the stairs when she saw all the people standing in the entry. "I—I'm sorry. I didn't know you had company."

When she started to turn, Dillon ran up the stairs and caught her elbow, then pulled her back down and introduced her to everyone.

"I didn't mean to intrude," she said politely. "I can talk to you about this later."

"About what?" Dillon reached for the frame Teresa held, then glanced at the picture. It was a photograph of his grandfather in full ceremonial dress, taken a year before his death. "This is my grandfather, Red Feather."

Teresa glanced at all the people staring at her, then quietly said, "He—he was with me. When I woke up after my delivery and they'd told me my baby had died. He was there. Watching over me, helping me."

At the stunned silence, Teresa blushed, then

swallowed hard. "I know it sounds crazy," she said quickly. "But it *was* him. I know it was. He was even wearing the same clothes."

Dillon looked at the picture again, saw the proud, weathered face of Red Feather staring back at him. A hot breeze kicked up, swirled through the open door, then softly died down.

A long silence settled over everyone in the entry, bringing with it the lingering sense of peace and harmony. Of balance.

"Ay, caramba." Maria bustled down the stairs and the peace dissolved like smoke in the wind. "Were you raised in a barn, Dillon Blackhawk? *Dios mio,* close the door and invite your company in."

The woman blew through the entryway, introducing herself while she herded everyone into the living room. Before Rebecca could get away, Dillon snatched her hand, then pulled her to him and gazed down at her. "Did you feel it?"

"Yes," she said, smiling. "I felt it."

"We're home, Rebecca," he whispered and lowered his mouth to hers. "At last, we're home."

SPOTLIGHT

Dying To Play

Debra Webb

When FBI agent Trace Callahan
arrives in Atlanta to investigate
a baffling series of multiple
homicides, deputy chief of
detectives Elaine Jentzen isn't
prepared for the immediate
attraction between them. And as
they hunt to find the killer known
as the Gamekeeper, it seems that
Trace is singled out as his next
victim...unless Elaine can stop the
Gamekeeper before it's too late.

Available January 2005.

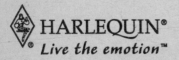

HARLEQUIN®
Live the emotion™

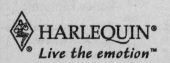

SAGA

USA TODAY **bestselling author**

JOAN ELLIOTT PICKART

**brings you a brand-new story in her
bestselling MacAllister family saga…**

MacAllister's Return

When Assistant D.A. Jesse Burke
finds out that he was stolen as a
baby, he heads to California to
discover his true heritage—and
finds unexpected love with
TV news anchor Krista Kelly.

**"Joan Elliott Pickart gives a delightful read via
inviting characters and a soft and light style."**
—*Romantic Times*

Coming in January 2005.

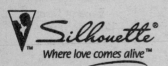

Where love comes alive™

**Exclusive
Bonus Features:**

**Author Interview
Sneak Preview…
and more!**